"Kiss Me!" He

Softly, she touched her lips to his. He increased the pressure until her mouth lost its shyness and became mobile. The swift heat of passion was all-consuming.

Abruptly, he drew her away. "Now I think I'd better take you home—"

"Dillon, I—"

He gave a harsh laugh. "We're not dealing on equal footing. I like to fight fair—"

"Fight?" Her eyes were wide. "Is this a fight?"

"The oldest kind," he returned, and suddenly his hand was firm under her chin. "It's not over, Laine, and when we have another round I may just say to the devil with the rules—"

NORA ROBERTS
lives with her family in the beautiful Blue Ridge Mountain range of western Maryland. She is an ardent sportswoman and an omnivorous reader, and has traveled the East Coast from Canada to Florida. She admits to being especially partial to spirited heroines and American settings, both of which are featured in her lively, contemporary romances.

Dear Reader:

I'd like to take this opportunity to thank you for all your support and encouragement of Silhouette Romances.

Many of you write in regularly, telling us what you like best about Silhouette, which authors are your favorites. This is a tremendous help to us as we strive to publish the best contemporary romances possible.

All the romances from Silhouette Books are for you, so enjoy this book and the many stories to come. I hope you'll continue to share your thoughts with us, and invite you to write to us at the address below:

Karen Solem
Editor-in-Chief
Silhouette Books
P.O. Box 769
New York, N.Y. 10019

NORA ROBERTS

Island of Flowers

Published by Silhouette Books New York
America's Publisher of Contemporary Romance

Other Silhouette Books by Nora Roberts

Irish Thoroughbred
Blithe Images
Song of the West
Search for Love

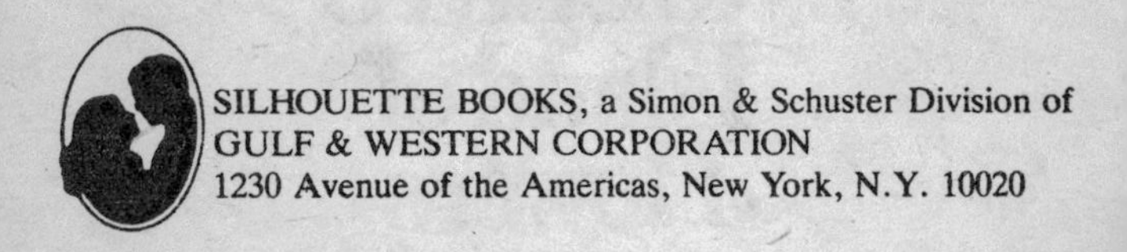
SILHOUETTE BOOKS, a Simon & Schuster Division of
GULF & WESTERN CORPORATION
1230 Avenue of the Americas, New York, N.Y. 10020

Distributed by Pocket Books

ISBN: 0-671-57180-X

First Silhouette Books printing October, 1982

10 9 8 7 6 5 4 3 2 1

Map by Ray Lundgren

America's Publisher of Contemporary Romance

Printed in the U.S.A.

Island of Flowers

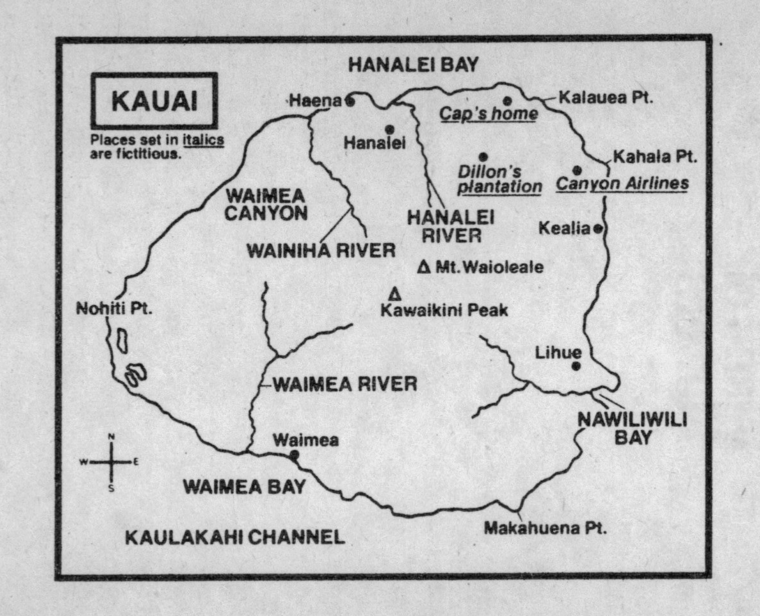
KAUAI
Places set in italics are fictitious.
HANALEI BAY
Haena
Hanalei
Cap's home
Kalauea Pt.
Kahala Pt.
Dillon's plantation
Canyon Airlines
WAIMEA CANYON
HANALEI RIVER
Kealia
WAINIHA RIVER
Δ Mt. Waioleale
Nohiti Pt.
Δ Kawaikini Peak
Lihue
WAIMEA RIVER
NAWILIWILI BAY
Waimea
N
W
E
S
WAIMEA BAY
Makahuena Pt.
KAULAKAHI CHANNEL

Chapter One

Laine's arrival at Honolulu International Airport was traditional. She would have preferred to melt through the crowd, but it appeared traveling tourist class categorized her as just that. Golden-skinned girls with ivory smiles and vivid sarongs bestowed brilliant colored leis. Accepting both kiss and floral necklace, Laine wove through the milling crowd and searched for an information desk. The girth of a fellow passenger hampered her journey. His yellow and orange flowered shirt and the twin cameras which joined the lei around his neck attested to his determination to enjoy his vacation. Under different circumstances, his appearance would have nudged at her humor, but the tension in Laine's stomach stifled any amusement. She had not stood on American soil in fifteen years. The ripe land with cliffs and beaches which she had seen as the plane descended brought no sense of homecoming.

The America Laine pictured came in sporadic patches of memory and through the perspective of a child of seven. America was a gnarled elm tree guarding her bedroom window. It was a spread of green grass where buttercups scattered gold. It was a mailbox at the end of a long, winding lane. But most of all, America was the man who had taken her to imaginary African jungles and desert islands. However, there were orchids instead of daisies. The graceful palms and spreading ferns of Honolulu were as foreign to Laine as the father she had traveled half the world to find. It seemed a lifetime ago that divorce had pulled her away from her roots.

Laine felt a quiet desperation that the address she had found among her mother's papers would lead to emptiness. The age of the small, creased piece of paper was unknown to her. Neither did she know if Captain James Simmons still lived on the island of Kauai. There had only been the address tossed in among her mother's bills. There had been no correspondence, nothing to indicate the address was still a vital one. To write to her father was the practical thing to do, and Laine had struggled with indecision for nearly a week. Ultimately, she had rejected a letter in favor of a personal meeting. Her horde of money would barely see her through a week of food and lodging, and though she knew the trip was impetuous, she had not been able to prevent herself. Threading through her doubts was the shimmering strand of fear that rejection waited for her at the end of her journey.

There was no reason to expect anything else, she lectured herself. *Why should the man who had left her fatherless during her growing-up years care about the woman she had become?* Relaxing the grip on the handle of her handbag, Laine reasserted her vow to accept whatever waited at her journey's end. She had learned long ago to adjust to whatever life offered. She concealed her feelings with the habit developed during her adolescence.

Quickly, she adjusted the white, soft-brimmed hat over a halo of flaxen curls. She lifted her chin. No one would have guessed her underlying anxiety as she moved with unconscious grace through the crowds. She looked elegantly aloof in her inherited traveling suit of ice blue silk, altered to fit her slight figure rather than her mother's ample curves.

The girl at the information desk was deep in an enjoyable conversation with a man. Standing to one side, Laine watched the encounter with detached interest. The man was dark and intimidatingly tall. Her pupils would undoubtedly have called him *séduisant*. His rugged features were surrounded by black hair in curling disorder, while his bronzed skin proved him no stranger to the Hawaiian sun. There was something rakish in his profile, some basic sensuality which Laine recognized but did not fully comprehend. She thought perhaps his nose had been broken at one time, but rather than spoiling the appeal of the profile, the lack of symmetry added to it. His dress was casual, the jeans well worn and frayed at the cuffs, and a denim work shirt exposed a hard chest and corded arms.

Vaguely irritated, Laine studied him. She observed the easy flow of charm, the indolent stance at the counter, the tease of a smile on his mouth. *I've seen his type before,* she thought with a surge of resentment, *hovering around Vanessa like crow around carrion.* She remembered, too, that when her mother's beauty had become only a shadow, the flock had left for younger prey. At that moment, Laine could feel only gratitude that her contacts with men had been limited.

He turned and encountered Laine's stare. One dark brow rose as he lingered over his survey of her. She was too unreasonably angry with him to look away. The simplicity of her suit shouted its exclusiveness, revealing the tender elegance of young curves. The hat half shaded a fragile, faintly aristocratic face with well-defined planes, straight nose, unsmiling mouth and morning-sky eyes.

Her lashes were thick and gold, and he took them as too long for authenticity. He assessed her as a cool, self-possessed woman, recognizing only the borrowed varnish.

Slowly, and with deliberate insolence, he smiled. Laine kept her gaze steady and struggled to defeat a blush. The clerk, seeing her companion's transfer of attention, shifted her eyes in Laine's direction and banished a scowl.

"May I help you?" Dutifully, she affixed her occupational smile. Ignoring the hovering male, Laine stepped up to the counter.

"Thank you. I need transportation to Kauai. Could you tell me how to arrange it?" A whisper of France lingered in her voice.

"Of course, there's a charter leaving for Kauai in . . ." The clerk glanced at her watch and smiled again. "Twenty minutes."

"I'm leaving right now." Laine glanced over and gave the loitering man a brief stare. She noted that his eyes were as green as Chinese jade. "No use hanging around the airport, and," he continued as his smile became a grin, "my Cub's not as crowded or expensive as the charter."

Laine's disdainful lift of brow and dismissing survey had been successful before, but did not work this time. "Do you have a plane?" she asked coldly.

"Yeah, I've got a plane." His hands were thrust in his pockets, and in his slouch against the counter, he still managed to tower over her. "I can always use the loose change from picking up island hoppers."

"Dillon," the clerk began, but he interrupted her with another grin and a jerk of his head.

"Rose'll vouch for me. I run for Canyon Airlines on Kauai." He presented Rose with a wide smile. She shuffled papers.

"Dillon . . . Mr. O'Brian is a fine pilot." Rose cleared her throat and sent Dillon a telling glance. "If you'd rather not wait for the scheduled charter, I can guarantee that your flight will be equally enjoyable with him."

Studying his irreverent smile and amused eyes, Laine was of the opinion that the trip would be something less than enjoyable. However, her funds were low and she knew she must conserve what she had.

"Very well, Mr. O'Brian, I will engage your services." He held out his hand, palm up, and Laine dropped her eyes to it. Infuriated by his rudeness, she brought her eyes back to his. "If you will tell me your rate, Mr. O'Brian, I shall be happy to pay you when we land."

"Your baggage check," he countered, smiling. "Just part of the service, lady."

Bending her head to conceal her blush, Laine fumbled through her purse for the ticket.

"O.K., let's go." He took both the stub and her arm, propelling her away as he called over his shoulder in farewell to the information clerk, "See you next time, Rose."

"Welcome to Hawaii," Rose stated out of habit, then with a sigh, pouted after Dillon's back.

Unused to being so firmly guided, and hampered by a stride a fraction of his, Laine struggled to maintain her composure while she trotted beside him. "Mr. O'Brian, I hope I don't have to jog to Kauai." He stopped and grinned at her. She tried, and failed, not to pant. His grin, she discovered, was a strange and powerful weapon, and one for which she had not yet developed a defense.

"Thought you were in a hurry, Miss . . ." He glanced at her ticket, and she watched the grin vanish. When his eyes lifted, all remnants of humor had fled. His mouth was grim. She would have retreated from the waves of hostility had not his grip on her arm prevented her. "Laine Simmons?" It was more accusation than question.

"Yes, you've read it correctly," she said.

Dillon's eyes narrowed. She found her cool façade melting with disconcerting speed. "You're going to see James Simmons?"

Her eyes widened. For an instant, a flash of hope flickered on her face. But his expression remained set and hostile. She smothered the impulse to ask hundreds of questions as she felt his tightening fingers bruise her arm.

"I don't know how that concerns you, Mr.

O'Brian," she began, "but yes. Do you know my father?" She faltered over the final word, finding the novelty of its use bittersweet.

"Yes, I know him . . . a great deal better than you do. Well, Duchess"—he released her as if the contact was offensive—"I doubt if fifteen years late is better than never, but we'll see. Canyon Airlines is at your disposal." He inclined his head and gave Laine a half bow. "The trip's on the house. I can hardly charge the owner's prodigal daughter." Dillon retrieved her luggage and stalked from the terminal in thunderous silence. In the wake of the storm, Laine followed, stunned by his hostility and by his information.

Her father owned an airline. She remembered James Simmons only as a pilot, with the dream of his own planes a distant fantasy. When had the dream become reality? Why did this man, who was currently tossing her mother's elegant luggage like so many duffel bags into a small, steamlined plane, turn such hostility on her at the discovery of her name? How did he know fifteen years had spanned her separation from her father? She opened her mouth to question Dillon as he rounded the nose of the plane. She shut it again as he turned and captured her with his angry stare.

"Up you go, Duchess. We've got twenty-eight minutes to endure each other's company." His hands went to her waist, and he hoisted her as if she were no more burden than a feather pillow. He eased his long frame into the seat beside her. She became uncomfortably aware of his virility and attempted to ignore him by giving intense concentration to the buckling of her safety belt. Beneath her lashes, she watched as he flicked at the controls before the engine roared to life.

The sea opened beneath them. Beaches lay white against its verge, dotted with sun worshipers. Mountains rose, jagged and primitive, the eternal rulers of the islands. As they gained height, the colors in the scene below became so intense that they seemed artificial. Soon the shades blended. Browns, greens and blues softened with distance. Flashes of scarlet and yellow merged before fading. The plane soared with a surge of power, then its wings tilted as it made a curving arch and hurtled into the sky.

"Kauai is a natural paradise," Dillon began in the tone of a tour guide. He leaned back in his seat and lit a cigarette. "It offers, on the North Shore, the Wailua River which ends at Fern Grotto. The foliage is exceptional. There are miles of beaches, fields of cane and pineapple. Opeakea Falls, Hanalei Bay and Na Pali Coast are also worth seeing. On the South Shore," he continued, while Laine adopted the air of attentive listener, "we have Kokie State Park and Waimea Canyon. There are tropical trees and flowers at Olopia and Menehune Gardens. Water sports are exceptional almost anywhere around the island. Why the devil did you come?"

The question, so abrupt on the tail of his mechanical recital, caused Laine to jolt in her seat and stare. "To . . . to see my father."

"Took your own sweet time about it," Dillon muttered and drew hard on his cigarette. He turned again and gave her a slow, intimate survey. "I guess you were pretty busy attending that elegant finishing school."

Laine frowned, thinking of the boarding school which had been both home and refuge for nearly fifteen years. She decided Dillon O'Brian was crazed. There was no use contradicting a lunatic. "I'm glad you approve," she returned coolly. "A pity you missed the experience. It's amazing what can be done with rough edges."

"No thanks, Duchess." He blew out a stream of smoke. "I prefer a bit of honest crudeness."

"You appear to have an adequate supply."

"I get by. Island life can be a bit uncivilized at times." His smile was thin. "I doubt if it's going to suit your tastes."

"I can be very adaptable, Mr. O'Brian." She moved her shoulders with gentle elegance. "I can also overlook a certain amount of discourtesy for short periods of time. Twenty-eight minutes is just under my limit."

"Terrific. Tell me, Miss Simmons," he continued with exaggerated respect, "how is life on the continent?"

"Marvelous." Deliberately, she tilted her head and looked at him from under the brim of her hat. "The French are so cosmopolitan, so urbane. One feels so . . ." Attempting to copy her mother's easy polish, she gestured and gave the next word the French expression. "*Chez soi* with people of one's own inclinations."

"Very true." The tone was ironic. Dillon kept his eyes on the open sky as he spoke. "I doubt if you'll find many people of your own inclinations on Kauai."

"Perhaps not." Laine pushed the thought of her father aside and tossed her head. "Then again, I may find the island as agreeable as I find Paris."

"I'm sure you found the men agreeable." Dillon crushed out his cigarette with one quick thrust. Laine found his fresh anger rewarding. The memory of the pitifully few men with whom she had had close contact caused her to force back a laugh. Only a small smile escaped.

"The men of my acquaintance"—she apologized mentally to elderly Father Rennier—"are men of elegance and culture and breeding. They are men of high intellect and discerning tastes who possess the manners and sensitivity which I currently find lacking in their American counterparts."

"Is that so?" Dillon questioned softly.

"That, Mr. O'Brian," said Laine firmly, "is quite so."

"Well, we wouldn't want to spoil our record." Switching over to automatic pilot, he turned in his seat and captured her. Mouth bruised mouth before she realized his intent.

She was locked in his arms, her struggles prevented by his strength and by her own dazed senses. She was overwhelmed by the scent and taste and feel of him. He increased the intimacy, parting her lips with his tongue. To escape from sensations more acute than she had thought possible, she clutched at his shirt.

Dillon lifted his face, and his brows drew straight at her look of stunned, young vulnerability. She could only stare, her eyes filled with confused new knowledge. Pulling away, he switched back to manual control and gave his attention to the sky. "It seems your French lovers haven't prepared you for American technique."

Stung, and furious with the weakness she had just discovered, Laine turned in her seat and faced him. "Your technique, Mr. O'Brian, is as crude as the rest of you."

He grinned and shrugged. "Be grateful, Duchess, that I didn't simply shove you out the door. I've been fighting the inclination for twenty minutes."

"You would be wise to suppress such inclinations," Laine snapped, feeling her temper bubbling at an alarming speed. *I will not lose it,* she told herself. She would not give this detestable man the satisfaction of seeing how thoroughly he had unnerved her.

The plane dipped into an abrupt nose dive. The sea hurtled toward them at a terrifying rate as the small steel bird performed a series of somersaults. The sky and sea were a mass of interchangeable blues with the white of clouds and the white of breakers no longer separate. Laine clutched at her seat, squeezing her eyes shut as the sea and sky whirled in her brain. Protest was impossible. She had lost both her voice and her heart at the first circle. She clung and prayed for her stomach to remain stationary. The plane leveled, then cruised rightside up, but inside her head the world still revolved. Laine heard her companion laugh wholeheartedly.

"You can open your eyes now, Miss Simmons. We'll be landing in a minute."

Turning to him, Laine erupted with a long, detailed analysis of his character. At length, she realized she was stating her opinion in French. She took a deep breath. "You, Mr. O'Brian," she finished in frigid English, "are the most detestable man I have ever met."

"Thank you, Duchess." Pleased, he began to hum.

Laine forced herself to keep her eyes open as Dillon began his descent. There was a brief impression of greens and browns melding with blue, and again the swift rise of mountains before they were bouncing on asphalt and gliding to a stop. Dazed, she surveyed the hangars and lines of aircraft, Piper Cubs and cabin planes, twin engines and passenger jets. *There's some mistake*, she thought. *This cannot belong to my father*.

"Don't get any ideas, Duchess," Dillon remarked, noting her astonished stare. His mouth tightened. "You've forfeited your share. And even if the Captain was inclined to be generous, his partner would make things very difficult. You're going to have to look someplace else for an easy ride."

He jumped to the ground as Laine stared at him with disbelief. Disengaging her belt, she prepared to lower herself to the ground. His hands gripped her waist before her feet made contact. For a moment, he held her suspended. With their faces only inches apart, Laine found his eyes her jailer. She had never known eyes so green or so compelling.

"Watch your step," he commanded, then dropped her to the ground.

Laine stepped back, retreating from the hostility in his voice. Gathering her courage, she lifted her chin and held her ground. "Mr.

O'Brian, would you please tell me where I might find my father."

He stared for a moment, and she thought he would simply refuse and leave her. Abruptly, he gestured toward a small white building. "His office is in there," he barked before he turned to stride away.

Chapter Two

The building which Laine approached was a mid-sized hut. Fanning palms and flaming anthurium skirted its entrance. Hands trembling, Laine entered. She felt as though her knees might dissolve under her, as though the pounding of her heart would burst through her head. What would she say to the man who had left her floundering in loneliness for fifteen years? What words were there to bridge the gap and express the need which had never died? Would she need to ask questions, or could she forget the whys and just accept?

Laine's image of James Simmons was as clear and vivid as yesterday. It was not dimmed by the shadows of time. *He would be older*, she reminded herself; *she was older as well*. She was not a child trailing after an idol, but a woman meeting her father. They were neither one the same as they had been. Perhaps that in itself would be an advantage.

The outer room of the hut was deserted. Laine had a vague impression of wicker furnishings and woven mats. She stared around her, feeling alone and unsure. Like a ghost of the past, his voice reached out, booming through an open doorway. Approaching the sound, Laine watched as her father talked on the phone at his desk.

She could see the alterations which age had made on his face, but her memory had been accurate. The sun had darkened his skin and laid its lines upon it, but his features were no stranger to her. His thick brows were gray now, but still prominent over his brown eyes. The nose was still strong and straight over the long, thin mouth. His hair remained full, though as gray as his brows, and she watched as he reached up in a well-remembered gesture and tugged his fingers through it.

She pressed her lips together as he replaced the receiver, then swallowing, Laine spoke in soft memory. "Hello, Cap."

He twisted his head, and she watched surprise flood his face. His eyes ran a quick gamut of emotions, and somewhere between the beginning and the end she saw the pain. He stood, and she noted with a small sense of shock that he was shorter than her child's perspective had made him.

"Laine?" The question was hesitant, colored by a reserve which crushed her impulse to rush toward him. She sensed immediately that his arms would not be open to receive her, and this rejection threatened to destroy her tentative smile.

"It's good to see you." Hating the inanity, she stepped into the room and held out her hand.

After a moment, he accepted it. He held her hand briefly, then released it. "You've grown up." His survey was slow, his smile touching only his mouth. "You've the look of your mother. No more pigtails?"

The smile illuminated her face with such swift impact, her father's expression warmed. "Not for some time. There was no one to pull them." Reserve settled over him again. Feeling the chill, Laine fumbled for some new line of conversation. "You've got your airport; you must be very happy. I'd like to see more of it."

"We'll arrange it." His tone was polite and impersonal, whipping across her face like the sting of a lash.

Laine wandered to a window and stared out through a mist of tears. "It's very impressive."

"Thank you, we're pretty proud of it." He cleared his throat and studied her back. "How long will you be in Hawaii?"

She gripped the windowsill and tried to match his tone. Even at their worst, her fears had not prepared her for this degree of pain. "A few weeks perhaps, I have no definite plans. I came . . . I came straight here." Turning, Laine began to fill the void with chatter. "I'm sure there are things I should see since I'm here. The pilot who flew me over said Kauai was beautiful, gardens and . . ." She tried and failed to remember the specifics of Dillon's speech. "And parks." She settled on a generality, keeping her smile fixed. "Perhaps you could recommend a hotel?"

He was searching her face, and Laine struggled to keep her smile from dissolving. "You're welcome to stay with me while you're here."

Burying her pride, she agreed. She knew she could not afford to stay anywhere else. "That's kind of you. I should like that."

He nodded and shuffled some papers on his desk. "How's your mother?"

"She died," Laine murmured. "Three months ago."

Cap glanced up sharply. Laine watched the pain flicker over his face. He sat down. "I'm sorry, Laine. Was she ill?"

"There was . . ." She swallowed. "There was a car accident."

"I see." He cleared his throat, and his tone was again impersonal. "If you had written, I would have flown over and helped you."

"Would you?" She shook her head and turned back to the window. She remembered the panic, the numbness, the mountain of debts, the auction of every valuable. "I managed well enough."

"Laine, why did you come?" Though his voice had softened, he remained behind the barrier of the desk.

"To see my father." Her words were devoid of emotion.

"Cap." At the voice Laine turned, watching as Dillon's form filled the doorway. His glance scanned her before returning to Cap. "Chambers is leaving for the mainland. He wants to see you before he takes off."

"All right. Laine," Cap turned and gestured awkwardly, "this is Dillon O'Brian, my partner. Dillon, this is my daughter."

"We've met." Dillon smiled briefly.

Laine managed a nod. "Yes, Mr. O'Brian was kind enough to fly me from Oahu. It was a most . . . fascinating journey."

"That's fine then." Cap moved to Dillon and clasped a hand to his shoulder. "Run Laine to the house, will you, and see she settles in? I'm sure she must be tired."

Laine watched, excluded from the mystery of masculine understanding as looks were exchanged. Dillon nodded. "My pleasure."

"I'll be home in a couple of hours." Cap turned and regarded Laine in awkward silence.

"All right." Her smile was beginning to hurt her cheeks, so Laine let it die. "Thank you." Cap hesitated, then walked through the door leaving her staring at emptiness. *I will not cry*, she ordered herself. *Not in front of this man*. If she had nothing else left, she had her pride.

"Whenever you're ready, Miss Simmons."

Brushing past Dillon, Laine glanced back over her shoulder. "I hope you drive a car with more discretion than you fly a plane, Mr. O'Brian."

He gave an enigmatic shrug. "Why don't we find out?"

Her bags were sitting outside. She glanced down at them, then up at Dillon. "You seem to have anticipated me."

"I had hoped," he began as he tossed the bags into the rear of a sleek compact, "to pack both them and you back to where you came from, but that is obviously impossible now." He opened his door, slid into the driver's seat and started the engine. Laine slipped in beside him, unaided. Releasing the brake, he shot forward with a speed which jerked her against the cushions.

"What did you say to him?" Dillon demanded, not bothering with preliminaries as he maneuvered skillfully through the airport traffic.

"Being my father's business partner does not entitle you to an account of his personal conversations with me," Laine answered. Her voice was clipped and resentful.

"Listen, Duchess, I'm not about to stand by while you drop into Cap's life and stir up trouble. I didn't like the way he looked when I walked in on you. I gave you ten minutes, and you managed to hurt him. Don't make me stop the car and persuade you to tell me." He paused and lowered his voice. "You'd find my methods unrefined." The threat vibrated in his softly spoken words.

Suddenly Laine found herself too tired to banter. Nights with only patches of sleep, days crowded with pressures and anxiety, and the long, tedious journey had taken their toll. With a weary gesture, she pulled off her hat. Resting her head against the seat, she closed her eyes. "Mr. O'Brian, it was not my intention to hurt my father. In the ten minutes you allowed, we said remarkably little. Perhaps it was the news that my mother had died which upset him, but that is something he would have learned eventually at any rate." Her tone was hollow, and he glanced at her, surprised by the sudden frailty of her unframed face. Her hair was soft and pale against her ivory skin. For the first time, he saw the smudges of mauve haunting her eyes.

"How long ago?"

Laine opened her eyes in confusion as she detected a whisper of sympathy in his voice. "Three months." She sighed and turned to face Dillon more directly. "She ran her car into a telephone pole. They tell me she died instantly." *And painlessly*, she added to herself, *anesthetized with several quarts of vintage champagne*.

Dillon lapsed into silence, and she was

grateful that he ignored the need for any trite words of sympathy. She had had enough of those already and found his silence more comforting. She studied his profile, the bronzed chiseled lines and unyielding mouth, before she turned her attention back to the scenery.

The scent of the Pacific lingered in the air. The water was a sparkling blue against the crystal beaches. Screw pines rose from the sand and accepted the lazy breeze, and monkeypods, wide and domelike, spread their shade in invitation. As they drove inland, Laine caught only brief glimpses of the sea. The landscape was a myriad of colors against a rich velvet green. Sun fell in waves of light, offering its warmth so that flowers did not strain to it, but rather basked lazily in its glory.

Dillon turned up a drive which was flanked by two sturdy palms. As they approached the house, Laine felt the first stir of pleasure. It was simple, its lines basic and clean, its walls cool and white. It stood two stories square, sturdy despite its large expanses of glass. Watching the windows wink in the sun, Laine felt her first welcoming.

"It's lovely."

"Not as fancy as you might have expected," Dillon countered as he halted at the end of the drive, "but Cap likes it." The brief truce was obviously at an end. He eased from the car and gave his attention to her luggage.

Without comment, Laine opened her door

and slipped out. Shading her eyes from the sun, she stood for a moment and studied her father's home. A set of stairs led to a circling porch. Dillon climbed them, nudged the front door open and strode into the house. Laine entered unescorted.

"Close my door; flies are not welcome."

Laine glanced up and saw, with stunned admiration, an enormous woman step as lightly down the staircase as a young girl. Her girth was wrapped in a colorful, flowing muumuu. Her glossy black hair was pulled tight and secured at the back of her head. Her skin was unlined, the color of dark honey. Her eyes were jet, set deep and widely spaced. Her age might have been anywhere from thirty to sixty. The image of an island priestess, she took a long, uninhibited survey of Laine when she reached the foot of the stairs.

"Who is this?" she asked Dillon as she folded her thick arms over a tumbling bosom.

"This is Cap's daughter." Setting down the bags, he leaned on the banister and watched the exchange.

"Cap Simmons's daughter." Her mouth pursed and her eyes narrowed. "Pretty thing, but too pale and skinny. Don't you eat?" She circled Laine's arm between her thumb and forefinger.

"Why, yes, I . . ."

"Not enough," she interrupted and fingered a sunlight curl with interest. "Mmm, very nice, very pretty. Why do you wear it so short?"

"I . . ."

"You should have come years ago, but you are here now." Nodding, she patted Laine's cheek. "You are tired. I will fix your room."

"Thank you. I . . ."

"Then you eat," she ordered, and hefted Laine's two cases up the stairs.

"That was Miri," Dillon volunteered and tucked his hands in his pockets. "She runs the house."

"Yes, I see." Unable to prevent herself, Laine lifted her hand to her hair and wondered over the length. "Shouldn't you have taken the bags up for her?"

"Miri could carry me up the stairs without breaking stride. Besides, I know better than to interfere with what she considers her duties. Come on." He grabbed her arm and pulled her down the hall. "I'll fix you a drink."

With casual familiarity, Dillon moved to a double-doored cabinet. Laine flexed her arm and surveyed the cream-walled room. Simplicity reigned here as its outer shell had indicated, and she appreciated Miri's obvious diligence with polish and broom. There was, she noted with a sigh, no room for a woman here. The furnishings shouted with masculinity, a masculinity which was well established and comfortable in its solitary state.

"What'll you have?" Dillon's question

brought Laine back from her musings. She shook her head and dropped her hat on a small table. It looked frivolous and totally out of place.

"Nothing, thank you."

"Suit yourself." He poured a measure of liquor into a glass and dropped down on a chair. "We're not given to formalities around here, Duchess. While you're in residence, you'll have to cope with a more basic form of existence."

She inclined her head, laying her purse beside her hat. "Perhaps one may still wash one's hands before dinner?"

"Sure," he returned, ignoring the sarcasm. "We're big on water."

"And where, Mr. O'Brian, do you live?"

"Here." He stretched his legs and gave a satisfied smile at her frown. "For a week or two. I'm having some repairs done to my house."

"How unfortunate," Laine commented and wandered the room. "For both of us."

"You'll survive, Duchess." He toasted her with his glass. "I'm sure you've had plenty of experience in surviving."

"Yes I have, Mr. O'Brian, but I have a feeling you know nothing about it."

"You've got guts, lady, I'll give you that." He tossed back his drink and scowled as she turned to face him.

"Your opinion is duly noted and filed."

"Did you come for more money? Is it possible you're that greedy?" He rose in one smooth motion and crossed the room, grabbing her shoulders before she could back away from his mercurial temper. "Haven't you squeezed enough out of him? Never giving anything in return. Never even disturbing yourself to answer one of his letters. Letting the years pile up without any acknowledgment. What the devil do you want from him now?"

Dillon stopped abruptly. The color had drained from her face, leaving it like white marble. Her eyes were dazed with shock. She swayed as though her joints had melted, and he held her upright, staring at her in sudden confusion. "What's the matter with you?"

"I . . . Mr. O'Brian, I think I would like that drink now, if you don't mind."

His frown deepened, and he led her to a chair before moving off to pour her a drink. Laine accepted with a murmured thanks, then shuddered at the unfamiliar burn of brandy. The room steadied, and she felt the mists clearing.

"Mr. O'Brian, I . . . am I to understand . . ." She stopped and shut her eyes a moment. "Are you saying my father wrote to me?"

"You know very well he did." The retort was both swift and annoyed. "He came to the islands right after you and your mother left him, and he wrote you regularly until five years ago when he gave up. He still sent money," Dillon added, flicking on his lighter.

"Oh yes, the money kept right on coming until you turned twenty-one last year."

"You're lying!"

Dillon looked over in astonishment as she rose from her chair. Her cheeks were flaming, her eyes flashing. "Well, well, it appears the ice maiden has melted." He blew out a stream of smoke and spoke mildly. "I never lie, Duchess. I find the truth more interesting."

"He never wrote to me. Never!" She walked to where Dillon sat. "Not once in all those years. All the letters I sent came back because he had moved away without even telling me where."

Slowly, Dillon crushed out his cigarette and rose to face her. "Do you expect me to buy that? You're selling to the wrong person, Miss Simmons. I saw the letters Cap sent, *and* the checks every month." He ran a finger down the lapel of her suit. "You seem to have put them to good use."

"I tell you I never received any letters." Laine knocked his hand away and tilted her head back to meet his eyes. "I have not had one word from my father since I was seven years old."

"Miss Simmons, I mailed more than one letter myself, though I was tempted to chuck them into the Pacific. Presents too; dolls in the early years. You must have quite a collection of porcelain dolls. Then there was the jewelry. I remember the eighteenth birthday present very clearly. Opal earrings shaped like flowers."

"Earrings," Laine whispered. Feeling the room tilt again she dug her teeth into her lip and shook her head.

"That's right." His voice was rough as he moved to pour himself another drink. "And they all went to the same place: seventeen rue de la Concorde, Paris."

Her color ebbed again, and she lifted a hand to her temple. "My mother's address," she murmured, and turned away to sit before her legs gave way. "I was in school; my mother lived there."

"Yes." Dillon took a quick sip and settled on the sofa again. "Your education was both lengthy and expensive."

Laine thought for a moment of the boarding school with its plain, wholesome food, cotton sheets and leaking roof. She pressed her fingers to her eyes. "I was not aware that my father was paying for my schooling."

"Just who did you think was paying for your French pinafores and art lessons?"

She sighed, stung by the sharpness of his tone. Her hands fluttered briefly before she dropped them into her lap. "Vanessa . . . my mother said she had an income. I never questioned her. She must have kept my father's letters from me."

Laine's voice was dull, and Dillon moved with sudden impatience. "Is that the tune you're going to play to Cap? You make it very convincing."

"No, Mr. O'Brian. It hardly matters at this point, does it? In any case, I doubt that he would believe me any more than you do. I will keep my visit brief, then return to France." She lifted her brandy and stared into the amber liquid, wondering if it was responsible for her numbness. "I would like a week or two. I would appreciate it if you would not mention this discussion to my father; it would only complicate matters."

Dillon gave a short laugh and sipped from his drink. "I have no intention of telling him any part of this little fairy tale."

"Your word, Mr. O'Brian." Surprised by the anxiety in her voice, Dillon glanced up. "I want your word." She met his eyes without wavering.

"My word, Miss Simmons," he agreed at length.

Nodding, she rose and lifted her hat and bag from the table. "I would like to go up to my room now. I'm very tired."

"Third door on your right."

He was frowning into his drink. Laine, without a backward glance, walked to her room.

Chapter Three

Laine faced the woman in the mirror. She saw a pale face, dominated by wide, shadowed eyes. Reaching for her rouge, she placed borrowed color in her cheeks.

She had known her mother's faults: the egotism, the shallowness. As a child, it had been easy to overlook the flaws and prize the sporadic, exciting visits with the vibrant, fairy-tale woman. Ice-cream parfaits and party dresses were such a contrast to homespun uniforms and porridge. As Laine had grown older, the visits had become further spaced and shorter. It became routine for her to spend her vacations from school with the nuns. She had begun to see, through the objectivity of distance, her mother's desperation for youth, her selfish grip on her own beauty. A grown daughter with firm limbs and unlined skin had been more of an obstacle than an accomplishment. A grown daughter was a reminder of one's own mortality.

She was always afraid of losing, Laine thought. Her looks, her youth, her friends, her men. All the creams and potions. She sighed and shut her eyes. All the dyes and lotions. There had been a collection of porcelain dolls, Laine remembered. Vanessa's dolls, or so she had thought. Twelve porcelain dolls, each from a different country. She thought of how beautiful the Spanish doll had been with its high comb and mantilla. And the earrings . . . Laine tossed down her brush and whirled around the room. Those lovely opal earrings that looked so fragile in Vanessa's ears. I remember seeing her wear them, just as I remember listing them and the twelve porcelain dolls for auction. *How much more that was mine did she keep from me*? Blindly, Laine stared out her window. The incredible array of island blossoms might not have existed.

What kind of woman was she to keep what was mine for her own pleasure? To let me think, year after year, that my father had forgotten me? She kept me from him, even from his words on paper. I resent her for that, how I resent her for that. Not for the money, but for the lies and the loss. She must have used the checks to keep her apartment in

Paris, and for all those clothes and all those parties. Laine shut her eyes tight on waves of outrage. At least I know now why she took me with her to France: as an insurance policy. She lived off me for nearly fifteen years, and even then it wasn't enough. Laine felt tears squeezing through her closed lids. Oh, how Cap must hate me. How he must hate me for the ingratitude and the coldness. He would never believe me. She sighed, remembering her father's reaction to her appearance. *"You've the look of your mother."* Opening her eyes, she walked back and studied her face in the mirror.

It was true, she decided as she ran her fingertips along her cheeks. The resemblance was there in the bone structure, in the coloring. Laine frowned, finding no pleasure in her inheritance. He's only to look at me to see her. He's only to look at me to remember. He'll think as Dillon O'Brian thinks. How could I expect anything else? For a few moments, Laine and her reflection merely stared at one another. But perhaps, she mused, her bottom lip thrust forward in thought, with a week or two I might salvage something of what used to be, some portion of the friendship. I would be content with that. But he must not think I've come for money, so I must be careful he not find out how little I have left. More than anything, I shall have to be careful around Mr. O'Brian.

Detestable man, she thought on a fresh

flurry of anger. He is surely the most ill-bred, mannerless man I have ever met. He's worse, much worse, than any of Vanessa's hangers-on. At least they managed to wear a light coat of respectability. Cap probably picked him up off the beach out of pity and made him his partner. He has insolent eyes, she added, lifting her brush and tugging it through her hair. Always looking at you as if he knew how you would feel in his arms. He's nothing but a womanizer. Tossing down the brush, she glared at the woman in the glass. He's just an unrefined, arrogant womanizer. Look at the way he behaved on the plane.

The glare faded as she lifted a finger to rub it over her lips. The memory of their turbulent capture flooded back. You've been kissed before, she lectured, shaking her head against the echoing sensations. *Not like that,* a small voice insisted. *Never like that.*

"Oh, the devil with Dillon O'Brian!" she muttered aloud, and just barely resisted the urge to slam her bedroom door on her way out.

Laine hesitated at the sound of masculine voices. It was a new sound for one generally accustomed to female company, and she found it pleasant. There was a mixture of deep blends, her father's booming drum tones and Dillon's laconic drawl. She heard a laugh, an appealing, uninhibited rumble, and she frowned as she recognized it as Dillon's. Quietly, she came down the rest of the steps and moved to the doorway.

"Then, when I took out the carburetor, he stared at it, muttered a stream of incantations and shook his head. I ended up fixing it myself."

"And a lot quicker than the Maui mechanic or any other would have." Cap's rich chuckle reached Laine as she stepped into the doorway.

They were seated easily. Dillon was sprawled on the sofa, her father in a chair. Pipe smoke rose from the tray beside him. Both were relaxed and so content in each other's company that Laine felt the urge to back away and leave them undisturbed. She felt an intruder into some long established routine. With a swift pang of envy, she took a step in retreat.

Her movement caught Dillon's attention. Before she could leave, his eyes held her motionless just as effectively as if his arms had reached out to capture her. She had changed from the sophisticated suit she had worn for the flight into a simple white dress from her own wardrobe. Unadorned and ingenue, it emphasized her youth and her slender innocence. Following the direction of Dillon's unsmiling survey, Cap saw Laine and rose. As he stood, his ease transformed into awkwardness.

"Hello, Laine. Have you settled in all right?"

Laine forced herself to shift her attention from Dillon to her father. "Yes, thank you."

The moistening of her lips was the first outward sign of nerves. "The room is lovely. I'm sorry. Did I interrupt?" Her hands fluttered once, then were joined loosely as if to keep them still.

"No . . . ah, come in and sit down. Just a little shop talk."

She hesitated again before stepping into the room.

"Would you like a drink?" Cap moved to the bar and jiggled glasses. Dillon remained silent and seated.

"No, nothing, thank you." Laine tried a smile. "Your home is beautiful. I can see the beach from my window." Taking the remaining seat on the sofa, Laine kept as much distance between herself and Dillon as possible. "It must be marvelous being close enough to swim when the mood strikes you."

"I don't get to the water as much as I used to." Cap settled down again, tapping his pipe against the tray. "Used to scuba some. Now, Dillon's the one for it." Laine heard the affection in his voice, and caught it again in his smiling glance at the man beside her.

"I find the sea and the sky have a lot in common," Dillon commented, reaching forward to lift his drink from the table. "Freedom and challenge." He sent Cap his easy smile. "I taught Cap to explore the fathoms, he taught me to fly."

"I suppose I'm more of a land creature," Laine replied, forcing herself to meet his gaze levelly. "I haven't much experience in the air or on the sea."

Dillon swirled his drink idly, but his eyes held challenge. "You do swim, don't you?"

"I manage."

"Fine." He took another swallow of his drink. "I'll teach you to snorkle." Setting down the glass, he resumed his relaxed position. "Tomorrow. We'll get an early start."

His arrogance shot up Laine's spine like a rod. Her tone became cool and dismissive. "I wouldn't presume to impose on your time, Mr. O'Brian."

Unaffected by the frost in her voice, Dillon continued, "No trouble. I've got nothing scheduled until the afternoon. You've got some extra gear around, haven't you, Cap?"

"Sure, in the back room." Hurt by the apparent relief in his voice, Laine shut her eyes briefly. "You'll enjoy yourself, Laine. Dillon's a fine teacher, and he knows these waters."

Laine gave Dillon a polite smile, hoping he could read between the lines. "I'm sure you know how much I appreciate your time, Mr. O'Brian."

The lifting of his brows indicated that their silent communication was proceeding with perfect understanding. "No more than I your company, Miss Simmons."

"Dinner." Miri's abrupt announcement startled Laine. "You." She pointed an accusing finger at Laine, then crooked it in a commanding gesture. "Come eat, and don't pick at your food. Too skinny," she muttered and whisked away in a flurry of brilliant colors.

Laine's arm was captured as they followed in the wake of Miri's waves. Dillon slowed her progress until they were alone in the corridor. "My compliments on your entrance. You were the picture of the pure young virgin."

"I have no doubt you would like to offer me to the nearest volcano god, Mr. O'Brian, but perhaps you would allow me to have my last meal in peace."

"Miss Simmons." He bowed with exaggerated gallantry and increased his hold on her arm. "Even I can stir myself on occasion to escort a lady into dinner."

"Perhaps with a great deal of concentration, you could accomplish this spectacular feat without breaking my arm."

Laine gritted her teeth as they entered the glass-enclosed dining room. Dillon pulled out her chair. She glanced coldly up at him. "Thank you, Mr. O'Brian," she murmured as she slid into her seat. Detestable man!

Inclining his head politely, Dillon rounded the table and dropped into a chair. "Hey, Cap, that little cabin plane we've been using on the Maui run is running a bit rough. I want to have a look at it before it goes up again."

"Hmm. What do you think's the problem?"

There began a technical, and to Laine unintelligible, discussion. Miri entered, placing a steaming tray of fish in front of Laine with a meaningful thump. To assure she had not been misunderstood, Miri pointed a finger at the platter, then at Laine's empty plate before she swirled from the room.

The conversation had turned to the intricacies of fuel systems by the time Laine had eaten all she could of Miri's fish. Her silence during the meal had been almost complete as the men enjoyed their mutual interest. She saw, as she watched him, that her father's lack of courtesy was not deliberate, but rather the result of years of living alone. He was, she decided, a man comfortable with men and out of his depth with feminine company. Though she felt Dillon's rudeness was intentional, it was her father's unconscious slight which stung.

"You will excuse me?" Laine rose during a brief lull in the conversation. She felt a fresh surge of regret as she read the discomfort in her father's eyes. "I'm a bit tired. Please." She managed a smile as she started to rise. "Don't disturb yourself, I know the way." As she turned to go, she could almost hear the room sigh with relief at her exit.

Later that evening, Laine felt stifled in her room. The house was quiet. The tropical moon had risen and she could see the curtains flutter with the gentle whispers of perfumed air. Unable to bear the loneliness of the four walls any longer, she stole quietly downstairs and into the night. As she wandered without regard for destination, she could hear the night birds call to each other, piercing the stillness with a strange, foreign music. She listened to the sea's murmur and slipped off her shoes to walk across the fine layer of sand to meet it.

The water fringed in a wide arch, frothing against the sands and lapping back into the womb of midnight blue. Its surface winked with mirrored stars. Laine breathed deeply of its scent, mingling with the flowered air.

But this paradise was not for her. Dillon and her father had banished her. It was the same story all over again. She remembered how often she had been excluded on her visits to her mother's home in Paris. *Again an intruder*, Laine decided, and wondered if she had either the strength or the will to pursue the smiling masquerade for even a week of her father's company. Her place was not with him any more than it had been with Vanessa. Dropping to the sand, Laine brought her knees to her chest and wept for the years of loss.

"I don't have a handkerchief, so you'll have to cope without one."

At the sound of Dillon's voice, Laine shuddered and hugged her knees tighter. "Please, go away."

"What's the problem, Duchess?" His voice was rough and impatient. If she had had more experience, Laine might have recognized a masculine discomfort with feminine tears. "If things aren't going as planned, sitting on the beach and crying isn't going to help. Especially if there's no one around to sympathize."

"Go away," she repeated, keeping her face buried. "I want you to leave me alone. I want to be alone."

"You might as well get used to it," he returned carelessly. "I intend to keep a close eye on you until you're back in Europe. Cap's too soft to hold out against the sweet, innocent routine for long."

Laine sprang up and launched herself at him. He staggered a moment as the small missile caught him off guard. "He's my father, do you understand? My *father*. I have a right to be with him. I have a right to know him." With useless fury, she beat her fists against his chest. He weathered the attack with some surprise before he caught her arms and dragged her, still swinging, against him.

"There's quite a temper under the ice! You can always try the routine about not getting his letters—that should further your campaign."

"I don't want his pity, do you hear?" She pushed and shoved and struck out while Dillon held her with minimum effort. "I would rather have his hate than his disinterest, but I would rather have his disinterest than his pity."

"Hold still, blast it," he ordered, losing patience with the battle. "You're going to get hurt."

"I will not hold still," Laine flung back. "I

am not a puppy who washed up on his doorstep and needs to be dried off and given a corner and a pat on the head. I *will* have my two weeks, and I won't let you spoil it for me." She tossed back her head. Tears fell freely, but her eyes now held fury rather than sorrow. "Let me go! I don't want you to touch me." She began to battle with new enthusiasm, kicking and nearly throwing them both onto the sand.

"All right, that's enough." Swiftly, he used his arms to band, his mouth to silence.

He was drawing her into a whirlpool, spinning and spinning, until all sense of time and existence was lost in the current. She would taste the salt of her own tears mixed with some tangy, vital flavor which belonged to him. She felt a swift heat rise to her skin and fought against it as desperately as she fought against his imprisoning arms. His mouth took hers once more, enticing her to give what she did not yet understand. All at once she lost all resistance, all sense of self. She went limp in his arms, her lips softening in surrender. Dillon drew her away and without even being aware of what she was doing, Laine dropped her head to his chest. She trembled as she felt his hand brush lightly through her hair, and nestled closer to him. Suddenly warm and no longer alone, she shut her eyes and let the gamut of emotions run its course.

"Just who are you, Laine Simmons?" Dillon drew her away again. He closed a firm hand under her chin as she stubbornly fought to keep her head lowered. "Look at me," he commanded. The order was absolute. With his eyes narrowed, he examined her without mercy.

Her eyes were wide and brimming, the tears trembling down her cheeks and clinging to her lashes. All layers of her borrowed sophistication had been stripped away, leaving only the vulnerability. His search ended on an impatient oath. "Ice, then fire, now tears. No, don't," he commanded as she struggled to lower her head again. "I'm not in the mood to test my resistance." He let out a deep breath and shook his head. "You're going to be nothing but trouble, I should have seen that from the first look. But you're here, and we're going to come to terms."

"Mr. O'Brian . . ."

"Dillon, for pity's sake. Let's not be any more ridiculous than necessary."

"Dillon," Laine repeated, sniffling and despising herself. "I don't think I can discuss terms with any coherence tonight. If you would just let me go, we could draw up a contract tomorrow."

"No, the terms are simple because they're all mine."

"That sounds exceedingly reasonable." She was pleased that irony replaced tears.

"While you're here," Dillon continued mildly, "we're going to be together like shadow and shade. I'm your guardian angel until you go back to the Left Bank. If you make a wrong move with Cap, I'm coming down on you so fast you won't be able to blink those little-girl eyes."

"Is my father so helpless he needs protection from his own daughter?" She brushed furiously at her lingering tears.

"There isn't a man alive who doesn't need protection from you, Duchess." Tilting his head, he studied her damp, glowing face. "If you're an operator, you're a good one. If you're not, I'll apologize when the time comes."

"You may keep your apology and have it for breakfast. With any luck, you'll strangle on it."

Dillon threw back his head and laughed, the same appealing rumble Laine had heard earlier. Outraged both with the laughter and its effect on her, she swung back her hand to slap his face.

"Oh, no." Dillon grabbed her wrist. "Don't spoil it. I'd just have to hit you back, and you look fabulous when you're spitting fire. It's much more to my taste than the cool mademoiselle from Paris. Listen, Laine." He took an exaggerated breath to control his laughter, and she found herself struggling to deal with the stir caused by the way her name sounded on his lips. "Let's try a truce, at least in public. Privately, we can have a round a night, with or without gloves."

"That should suit you well enough." Laine wriggled out of his loosened hold and tossed her head. "You have a considerable advantage—given your weight and strength."

"Yeah." Dillon grinned and moved his shoulders. "Learn to live with it. Come on." He took her hand in a friendly gesture which nonplussed her. "Into bed; you've got to get up early tomorrow. I don't like to lose the morning."

"I'm not going with you tomorrow." She tugged her hand away and planted her bare heels in the sand. "You'll probably attempt to drown me, then hide my body in some cove."

Dillon sighed in mock exasperation. "Laine, if I have to drag you out of bed in the morning, you're going to find yourself learning a great deal more than snorkeling. Now, are you going to walk back to the house, or do I carry you?"

"If they could bottle your arrogance, Dillon O'Brian, there would be no shortage of fuel in this country!"

With this, Laine turned and fled. Dillon watched until the darkness shrouded her white figure. Then he bent down to retrieve her shoes.

Chapter Four

The morning was golden. As usual, Laine woke early. For a moment, she blinked in puzzlement. Cool green walls had replaced her white ones, louvered shades hung where she expected faded striped curtains. Instead of her desk stood a plain mahogany bureau topped with a vase of scarlet blossoms. But it was the silence which most confused her. There were no giggles, no rushing feet outside her door. The quiet was broken only by a bird who sang his morning song outside her window. Memory flooded back. With a sigh, Laine lay back against the pillow and wished she could go to sleep again. The habit of early rising was too ingrained. She rose, showered and dressed.

A friend had persuaded her to accept the

loan of a swimsuit, and Laine studied the two tiny pieces. She slipped on what had been described as a modified bikini. The silvery blue was flattering, highlighting her subtle curves, but no amount of adjustment could result in a more substantial coverage. There was definitely too much of her and too little suit.

"Silly," Laine muttered and adjusted the halter strings a last time. "Women wear these things all the time, and I've hardly the shape for drawing attention."

Skinny. With a grimace, she recalled Miri's judgment. Laine gave the top a last, hopeless tug. I don't think all the fish in the Pacific are going to change this inadequacy. Pulling on white jeans and a scarlet scoop-necked top, she reminded herself that cleavage was not what she needed for dealing with Dillon O'Brian.

As she wandered downstairs, Laine heard the stirrings which accompany an awakening house. She moved quietly, half afraid she would disturb the routine. In the dining room, the sun poured like liquid gold through the windows. Standing in its pool, Laine stared out at soft ferns and brilliant poppies. Charmed by the scene, she decided she would let nothing spoil the perfection of the day. There would be time enough later, on some drizzling French morning, to think of rejections and humiliations, but today the sun was bright and filled with promise.

"So, you are ready for breakfast." Miri glided in from the adjoining kitchen. She managed to look graceful despite her size, and regal despite the glaring flowered muumuu.

"Good morning, Miri." Laine gave her the first smile of the day and gestured toward the sky. "It's beautiful."

"It will bring some color to your skin." Miri sniffed and ran a finger down Laine's arm. "Red if you aren't careful. Now, sit and I will put flesh on your skinny bones." Imperiously, she tapped the back of a chair, and Laine obeyed.

"Miri, have you worked for my father long?"

"Ten years." Miri shook her head and poured steaming coffee into a cup. "Too long a time for a man not to have a wife. Your mother," she continued, narrowing her dark eyes, "she was skinny too?"

"Well, no, I wouldn't say . . . That is . . ." Laine hesitated in an attempt to gauge Miri's estimation of a suitable shape.

Rich laughter shot out. Miri's bosom trembled under pink and orange flowers. "You don't want to say she was not as much woman as Miri." She ran her hands over her well-padded hips. "You're a pretty girl," she said unexpectedly and patted Laine's flaxen curls. "Your eyes are too young to be sad." As Laine stared up at her, speechless under the unfamiliar affection, Miri sighed. "I will bring your breakfast, and you will eat what I give you."

"Make it two, Miri." Dillon strolled in, bronzed and confident in cut-off denims and a plain white T-shirt. "Morning, Duchess. Sleep well?" He dropped into the chair opposite Laine and poured himself a cup of coffee. His movements were easy, without any early morning lethargy, and his eyes were completely alert. Laine concluded that Dillon O'Brian was one of those rare creatures who moved from sleep to wakefulness instantly. It also occurred to her, in one insistent flash, that he was not only the most attractive man she had ever known, but the most compelling. Struggling against an unexplained longing, Laine tried to mirror his casualness.

"Good morning, Dillon. It appears it's going to be another lovely day."

"We've a large supply of them on this side of the island."

"On this side?" Laine watched as he ran a hand through his hair, sending it into a state of appealing confusion.

"Mmm. On the windward slopes it rains almost every day." He downed half his coffee in one movement, and Laine found herself staring at his long, brown fingers. They looked strong and competent against the cream-colored earthenware. Suddenly, she remembered the feel of them on her chin. "Something wrong?"

"What?" Blinking, she brought her attention back to his face. "No, I was just thinking . . . I'll have to tour the island while I'm here," she improvised, rushing through the words. "Is your . . . is your home near here?"

"Not far." Dillon lifted his cup again, studying her over its rim. Laine began to stir her own coffee as if the task required enormous concentration. She had no intention of drinking it, having had her first—and, she vowed, last—encounter with American coffee aboard the plane.

"Breakfast," Miri announced, gliding into the room with a heaping tray. "You will eat." With brows drawn, she began piling portions onto Laine's plate. "And then you go out so I can clean my house. You!" She shook a large spoon at Dillon who was filling his own plate with obvious appreciation. "Don't bring any sand back with you to dirty my floors."

He responded with a quick Hawaiian phrase and a cocky grin. Miri's laughter echoed after her as she moved from the room and into the kitchen.

"Dillon," Laine began, staring at the amount of food on her plate, "I could never eat all of this."

He forked a mouthful of eggs and shrugged. "Better make a stab at it. Miri's decided to fatten you up, and even if you couldn't use it—and you can," he added as he buttered a piece of toast, "Miri is not a lady to cross. Pretend it's bouillabaisse or escargot."

The last was stated with a tangible edge, and Laine stiffened. Instinctively, she put up her defenses. "I have no complaints on the quality of the food, but on the quantity."

Dillon shrugged. Annoyed, Laine attacked her breakfast. The meal progressed without conversation. Fifteen minutes later, she searched for the power to lift yet another forkful of eggs. With a sound of impatience, Dillon rose and pulled her from her chair.

"You look like you'll keel over if you shovel in one more bite. I'll give you a break and get you out before Miri comes back."

Laine gritted her teeth, hoping it would help her to be humble. "Thank you."

As Dillon pulled Laine down the hall toward the front door, Cap descended the stairs. All three stopped as he glanced down from man to woman. "Good morning. It should be a fine day for your snorkeling lesson, Laine."

"Yes, I'm looking forward to it." She smiled, straining for a naturalness she was unable to feel in his presence.

"That's good. Dillon's right at home in the water." Cap's smile gained warmth as he turned to the man by her side. "When you come in this afternoon, take a look at the new twin engine. I think the modifications you specified worked out well."

"Sure. I'm going to do a bit of work on that cabin plane. Keep Tinker away from it, will you?"

Cap chuckled as they enjoyed some personal joke. When he turned to Laine, he had a remnant of his smile and a polite nod. "I'll see you tonight. Have a good time."

"Yes, thank you." She watched him move away and, for a moment, her heart lifted to her eyes. Looking back, she found Dillon studying her. His expression was indrawn and brooding.

"Come on," he said with sudden briskness as he captured her hand. "Let's get started." He lifted a faded, long-stringed bag and tossed it over his shoulder as they passed through the front door. "Where's your suit?"

"I have it on." Preferring to trot alongside rather than be dragged, Laine scrabbled to keep pace.

The path he took was a well-worn dirt track. Along its borders, flowers and ferns crept to encroach on the walkway. Laine wondered if there was another place on earth where colors had such clarity or where green had so many shades. The vanilla-scented blossoms of heliotrope added a tang to the moist sea air. With a high call, a skylark streaked across the sky and disappeared. Laine and Dillon walked in silence as the sun poured unfiltered over their heads.

After a ten minute jog, Laine said breathlessly, "I do hope it isn't much farther. I haven't run the decathlon for years."

Dillon turned, and she braced herself for his irritated retort. Instead, he began to walk at a more moderate pace. Pleased, Laine allowed herself a small smile. She felt even a minor victory in dealing with Dillon O'Brian was an accomplishment. Moments later, she forgot her triumph.

The bay was secluded, sheltered by palms and laced with satin-petaled hibiscus. In the exotic beauty of Kauai, it was a stunning diamond. The water might have dripped from the sky that morning. It shone and glimmered like a multitude of fresh raindrops.

With a cry of pleasure, Laine began to pull Dillon through the circling palms and into the white heat of sun and sand. "Oh, it's beautiful!" She turned two quick circles as if to insure encompassing all the new wonders. "It's perfect, absolutely perfect."

She watched his smile flash like a brisk wind. It chased away the clouds and, for one precious moment, there was understanding rather than tension between them. It flowed from man to woman with an ease which was as unexpected as it was soothing. His frown returned abruptly, and Dillon crouched to rummage through the bag. He pulled out snorkels and masks.

"Snorkeling's easy once you learn to relax and breathe properly. It's important to be both relaxed and alert." He began to instruct in simple terms, explaining breathing techniques and adjusting Laine's mask.

"There is no need to be quite so didactic," she said at length, irked by his patronizing tone and frowning face. "I assure you, I have a working brain. Most things don't have to be repeated more than four or five times before I grasp the meaning."

"Fine." He handed her both snorkel and mask. "Let's try it in the water." Pulling off his shirt, he dropped it on the canvas bag. He stood above her adjusting the strap on his own mask.

A fine mat of black hair lay against his bronzed chest. His skin was stretched tight over his rib cage, then tapered down to a narrow waist. The faded denim hung low over his lean hips. With some astonishment, Laine felt an ache start in her stomach and move warmly through her veins. She dropped her eyes to an intense study of the sand.

"Take off your clothes." Laine's eyes widened. She took a quick step in retreat. "Unless you intend to swim in them." Dillon added. His lips twitched before he turned and moved toward the water.

Embarrassed, Laine did her best to emulate his casualness. Shyly, she stripped off her top. Pulling off her jeans, she folded both and followed Dillon toward the bay. He waited for her, water lapping over his thighs. His eyes traveled over every inch of her exposed skin before they rested on her face.

"Stay close," he commanded when she stood beside him. "We'll skim the surface for a bit until you get the hang of it." He pulled the mask down over her eyes and adjusted it.

Easily, they moved along the shallows where sunlight struck the soft bottom and sea lettuce danced and swayed. Forgetting her instructions, Laine breathed water instead of air and surfaced choking.

"What happened?" Dillon demanded, as Laine coughed and sputtered. "You're going to have to pay more attention to what you're doing," he warned. Giving her a sturdy thump on the back, he pulled her mask back over her eyes. "Ready?" he asked.

After three deep breaths, Laine managed to speak. "Yes." She submerged.

Little by little, she explored deeper water, swimming by Dillon's side. He moved through the water as a bird moves through the air, with inherent ease and confidence. Before long, Laine learned to translate his aquatic hand signals and began to improvise her own. They were joined in the liquid world by curious fish. As Laine stared into round, lidless eyes, she wondered who had come to gape at whom.

The sun flickered through with ethereal light. It nurtured the sea grass and caused shells and smooth rocks to glisten. It was a silent world, and although the sea bottom teemed with life, it was somehow private and free. Pale pink fingers of coral grouped together to form a hiding place for vivid blue fish. Laine watched in fascination as a hermit crab slid out of its borrowed shell and scurried away. There was a pair of orange starfish clinging contentedly to a rock, and a sea urchin nestled in spiny solitude.

Laine enjoyed isolation with this strange, moody man. She did not pause to appraise the pleasure she took in sharing her new experiences with him. The change in their relationship had been so smooth and so swift, she had not even been aware of it. They were, for a moment, only man and woman cloaked in a world of water and sunlight. On impulse, she lifted a large cone-shaped shell from its bed, its resident long since evicted. First holding it out for Dillon to view, she swam toward the dancing light on the surface.

Shaking her head as she broke water, Laine splattered Dillon's mask with sun drops. Laughing, she pushed her own mask to the top of her head and stood in the waist-high water. "Oh, that was wonderful! I've never seen anything like it." She pushed damp tendrils behind her ears. "All those colors, and so many shades of blue and green molded together. It feels . . . it feels as if there were nothing else in the world but yourself and where you are."

Excitement had kissed her cheeks with color, her eyes stealing the blue from the sea. Her hair was dark gold, clinging in a sleek cap to her head. Now, without the softening of curls, her face seemed more delicately sculptured, the planes and hollows more fragile. Dillon watched her in smiling silence, pushing his own mask atop his head.

"I've never done anything like that before. I could have stayed down there forever. There's so much to see, so much to touch. Look what I found. It's beautiful." She held the shell in both hands, tracing a finger over its amber lines. "What is it?"

Dillon took it for a moment, turning it over in his hands before giving it back to her. "A music volute. You'll find scores of shells around the island."

"May I keep it? Does this place belong to anyone?"

Dillon laughed, enjoying her enthusiasm. "This is a private bay, but I know the owner. I don't think he'd mind."

"Will I hear the sea? They say you can." Laine lifted the shell to her ear. At the low, drifting echo, her eyes widened in wonder. *"Oh, c'est incroyable."* In her excitement, she reverted to French, not only in speech, but in mannerisms. Her eyes locked on his as one hand held the shell to her ear and the other gestured with her words. *"On entende le bruit de la mer. C'est merveilleux!* Dillon, *ećoute."*

She offered the shell, wanting to share her discovery. He laughed as she had heard him laugh with her father. "Sorry, Duchess, you lost me a few sentences back."

"Oh, how silly. I wasn't thinking. I haven't spoken English in so long." She brushed at her damp hair and offered him a smile. "It's marvelous, I can really hear the sea." Her words faltered as his eyes lost their amusement. They were darkened by an emotion which caused her heart to jump and pound furiously against her ribs. Her mind shouted quickly to retreat, but her body and will melted as his arms slid around her. Her mouth lifted of its own accord to surrender to his.

For the first time, she felt a man's hands roam over her naked skin. There was nothing between them but the satin rivulets of water which clung to their bodies. Under the streaming gold sun, her heart opened, and she gave. She accepted the demands of his mouth, moved with the caresses of his hands until she thought they would never become separate. She wanted only for them to remain one until the sun died, and the world was still.

Dillon released her slowly, his arms lingering, as if reluctant to relinquish possession. Her sigh was mixed with pleasure and the despair of losing a newly discovered treasure. "I would swear," he muttered, staring down into her face, "you're either a first-rate actress or one step out of a nunnery."

Immediately, the helpless color rose, and Laine turned to escape to the sand of the beach. "Hold on." Taking her arm, Dillon turned her to face him. His brows drew close as he studied her blush. "That's a feat I haven't seen in years. Duchess, you amaze me. Either way," he continued, and his smile held mockery but lacked its former malice, "calculated or innocent, you amaze me.

Again," he said simply and drew her into his arms.

This time the kiss was gentle and testing. But she had less defense against tenderness than passion, and her body was pliant to his instruction. Her hands tightened on his shoulders, feeling the ripple of muscles under her palms as he drew every drop of response from her mouth. With no knowledge of seduction, she became a temptress by her very innocence. Dillon drew her away and gave her clouded eyes and swollen mouth a long examination.

"You're a powerful lady," he said at length, then let out a quick breath. "Let's sit in the sun awhile." Without waiting for her answer, he took her hand and moved toward the beach.

On the sand, he spread a large beach towel and dropped onto it. When Laine hesitated, he pulled her down to join him. "I don't bite, Laine, I only nibble." Drawing a cigarette from the bag beside them, he lit it, then leaned back on his elbows. His skin gleamed with water and sun.

Feeling awkward, Laine sat very still with the shell in her hands. She tried not only to understand what she had felt in Dillon's arms, but why she had felt it. It had been important, and somehow, she felt certain it would remain important for the rest of her life. It was a gift that did not yet have a name. Suddenly, she felt as happy as when the shell had spoken in her ear. Glancing at it, Laine smiled with unrestrained joy.

"You treat that shell as though it were your firstborn." Twisting her head, she saw Dillon grinning. She decided she had never been happier.

"It is my first souvenir, and I've never dived for sunken treasure before."

"Just think of all the sharks you had to push out of the way to get your hands on it." He blew smoke at the sky as she wrinkled her nose at him.

"Perhaps you're jealous because you didn't get one of your own. I suppose it was selfish of me not to have gotten one for you."

"I'll survive."

"You don't find shells in Paris," she commented, feeling at ease and strangely fresh. "The children will treasure it as much as they would gold doubloons."

"Children?"

Laine was examining her prize, exploring its smooth surface with her fingers. "My students at school. Most of them have never seen anything like this except in pictures."

"You teach?"

Much too engrossed in discovering every angle of the shell, Laine missed the incredulity in his voice. She answered absently, "Yes, English to the French students and French to the English girls who board there. After I graduated, I stayed on as staff. There was really nowhere else to go, and it had always been home in any case. Dillon, do you suppose I could come back sometime and find one or two others, a different type perhaps? The girls would be fascinated; they get so little entertainment."

"Where was your mother?"

"What?" In the transfer of her attention, she saw he was sitting up and staring at her with hard, probing eyes. "What did you say?" she asked again, confused by his change of tone.

"I said, where was your mother?"

"When . . . when I was in school? She was in Paris." The sudden anger in his tone threw her into turmoil. She searched for a way to change the topic. "I would like to see the airport again; do you think I . . ."

"Stop it."

Laine jerked at the harsh command, then quickly tried to slip into her armor. "There's no need to shout. I'm quite capable of hearing you from this distance."

"Don't pull that royal routine on me, Duchess. I want some answers." He flicked away his cigarette. Laine saw both the determination and fury in his face.

"I'm sorry, Dillon." Rising and stepping out of reach, Laine remained outwardly calm. "I'm really not in the mood for a cross-examination."

With a muttered oath, Dillon swung to his feet and captured her arms with a swiftness which left her stunned. "You can be a frosty little number. You switch on and off so fast, I can't make up my mind which is the charade. Just who the devil are you?"

"I'm tired of telling you who I am," she answered quietly. "I don't know what you want me to say; I don't know what you want me to be."

Her answer and her mild tone seemed only to make him more angry. He tightened his hold and gave her a quick shake. "What was this last routine of yours?"

She was yanked against him in a sudden blaze of fury, but before punishment could be meted out, someone called his name. With a soft oath Dillon released her, and turned as a figure emerged from a narrow tunnel of palms.

Laine's first thought was that a spirit from the island was drifting through the shelter and across the sand. Her skin was tawny gold and smooth against a sarong of scarlet and midnight blue. A full ebony carpet of hair fell to her waist, flowing gently with her graceful movements. Almond-shaped amber eyes were fringed with dark velvet. A sultry smile flitted across an exotic and perfect face. She lifted a hand in greeting, and Dillon answered.

"Hello, Orchid."

Her mortality was established in Laine's mind as the beautiful apparition lifted her lips and brushed Dillon's. "Miri said you'd gone snorkeling, so I knew you'd be here." Her voice flowed like soft music.

"Laine Simmons, Orchid King." Dillon's introductions were casual. Laine murmured a response, feeling suddenly as inadequate as a shadow faced with the sun. "Laine's Cap's daughter."

"Oh, I see." Laine was subjected to a more lengthy survey. She saw speculation beneath the practiced smile. "How nice you're visiting at last. Are you staying long?"

"A week or two." Laine regained her poise and met Orchid's eyes. "Do you live on the island?"

"Yes, though I'm off it as often as not. I'm a flight attendant. I'm just back from the mainland, and I've got a few days. I wanted to trade the sky for the sea. I hope you're going back in." She smiled up at Dillon and tucked a hand through his arm. "I would love some company."

Laine watched his charm flow. It seemed he need do nothing but smile to work his own particular magic. "Sure, I've got a couple of hours."

"I think I'll just go back to the house," Laine said quickly, feeling like an intruder. "I don't think I should get too much sun at one time." Lifting her shirt, Laine tugged it on. "Thank you, Dillon, for your time." She bent down and retrieved the rest of her things before speaking again. "It's nice to have met you, Miss King."

"I'm sure we'll see each other again." Undraping her sarong, Orchid revealed an inadequate bikini and a stunning body. "We're all very friendly on the island, aren't we, cousin?" Though it was the standard island form of address, Orchid's use of the word cousin implied a much closer relationship.

"Very friendly." Dillon agreed with such ease that Laine felt he must be quite accustomed to Orchid's charms.

Murmuring a goodbye, Laine moved toward the canopy of palms. Hearing Orchid laugh, then speak in the musical tongue of the island, Laine glanced back before the leaves blocked out the view. She watched the golden arms twine around Dillon's neck, pulling his mouth toward hers in invitation.

Chapter Five

The walk back from the bay gave Laine time to reflect on the varying emotions Dillon O'Brian had managed to arouse in the small amount of time she had known him. Annoyance, resentment and anger had come first. Now, there was a wariness she realized stemmed from her inexperience with men. But somehow, that morning, there had been a few moments of harmony. She had been at ease in his company. And, she admitted ruefully, she had never before been totally at ease in masculine company on a one-to-one basis.

Perhaps it had simply been the novelty of her underwater adventure which had been responsible for her response to him. There had been something natural in their coming together, as if body had been created for body and mouth for mouth. She had felt a freedom in his arms, an awakening. It had been as if walls of glass had shattered and left her open to sensations for the first time.

Stopping, Laine plucked a blush pink hibiscus, then twirled its stem idly as she wandered up the dirt track. Her tenuous feelings had been dissipated first by Dillon's unexplained anger, then by the appearance of the dark island beauty.

Orchid King, Laine mused. A frown marred her brow as the name of the flirtatious information clerk ran through her brain. *Rose.* Smoothing the frown away, Laine shook off a vague depression. Perhaps Dillon had a predilection for women with flowery names. It was certainly none of her concern. Obviously, she continued, unconsciously tearing off the hibiscus petals, he gave and received kisses as freely as a mouse nibbles cheese. He simply kissed me because I was there. Obviously, she went on doggedly, shredding the wounded blossom without thought, Orchid King has a great deal more to offer than I. She makes me feel like a pale, shapeless wren next to a lush, vibrant flamingo. I would hardly appeal to him as a woman even if he didn't already dislike me. I don't want to appeal to him. Certainly not. The very last thing I want to do is to appeal to that insufferable man. Scowling, she stared down at the mutilated hibiscus. With something between a sigh and a moan, she tossed it aside and increased her pace.

After depositing the shell in her room and changing out of her bathing suit, Laine wandered back downstairs. She felt listless and at loose ends. In the organized system of classes and meals and designated activities, her time had always been carefully budgeted. She found the lack of demand unsettling. She thought of how often during the course of a busy day she had yearned for a free hour to read or simply to sit alone. Now her time was free, and she wished only for occupation. The difference was, she knew, the fear of idle hours and the tendency to think. She found herself avoiding any attempt to sort out her situation or the future.

No one had shown her through the house since her arrival. After a brief hesitation, she allowed curiosity to lead her and gave herself a tour. She discovered that her father lived simply, with no frills or frippery, but with basic masculine comforts. There were books, but it appeared they were little read. She could see by the quantity and ragged appearance of aeronautical magazines where her father's taste in literature lay. Bamboo shades replaced conventional curtains; woven mats took the place of rugs. While far from primitive, the rooms were simply furnished.

Her mind began to draw a picture of a man content with such a basic existence, who lived quietly and routinely; a man whose main outlet was his love of the sky. Now Laine began to understand why her parents' marriage had failed. Her father's life-style was as unassuming as her mother's had been pretentious. Her mother would never have been satisfied with her father's modest existence, and he would have been lost in hers. Laine wondered, with a small frown, why she herself did not seem to fit with either one of them.

Laine lifted a black-framed snapshot from a desk. A younger version of Cap Simmons beamed out at her, his arm casually tossed around a Dillon who had not yet reached full manhood. Dillon's smile was the same, however—somewhat cocky and sure. If they had stood in the flesh before her, their affection for each other would have seemed no less real. A shared understanding was revealed in their eyes and their easy stance together. It struck Laine suddenly, with a stab of resentment, that they looked like father and son. The years they had shared could never belong to her.

"It's not fair," she murmured, gripping the picture in both hands. With a faint shudder, she shut her eyes. Who am I blaming? she asked herself. Cap for needing someone? Dillon for being here? Blame won't help, and looking for the past is useless. It's time I looked for something new. Letting out a deep breath, Laine replaced the photograph. She turned away and moved further down the hall. In a moment, she found herself in the kitchen surrounded by gleaming white appliances and hanging copper kettles. Miri turned from the stove and gave Laine a satisfied smile.

"So, you have come for lunch." Miri tilted her head and narrowed her eyes. "You have some color from the sun."

Laine glanced down at her bare arms and was pleased with the light tan. "Why yes, I do. I didn't actually come for lunch though." She smiled and made an encompassing gesture. "I was exploring the house."

"Good. Now you eat. Sit here." Miri waved a long knife toward the scrubbed wooden table. "And do not make your bed anymore. That is my job." Miri plopped a glass of milk under Laine's nose, then gave a royal sniff.

"Oh, I'm sorry." Laine glanced from the glass of milk up to Miri's pursed lips. "It's just a habit."

"Don't do it again," Miri commanded as she turned to the refrigerator. She spoke again as she began to remove a variety of contents. "Did you make beds in that fancy school?"

"It isn't actually a fancy school," Laine corrected, watching with growing anxiety as Miri prepared a hefty sandwich. "It's really just a small convent school outside Paris."

"You lived in a convent?" Miri stopped her sandwich building and looked skeptical.

"Well, no. That is, one might say I lived on the fringes of one. Except, of course, when I visited my mother. Miri . . ." Daunted by the plate set in front of her, Laine looked up helplessly. "I don't think I can manage all this."

"Just eat, Skinny Bones. Your morning with Dillon, it was nice?"

"Yes, very nice." Laine applied herself to the sandwich as Miri eased herself into the opposite chair. "I never knew there was so much to see underwater. Dillon is an expert guide."

"Ah, that one." Miri shook her head and somehow categorized Dillon as a naughty twelve-year-old boy. "He is always in the water or in the sky. He should keep his feet planted on the ground more often." Leaning back, Miri kept a commanding eye on Laine's progress. "He watches you."

"Yes, I know," Laine murmured. "Like a parole officer. I met Miss King," she continued, lifting her voice. "She came to the bay."

"Orchid King." Miri muttered something in unintelligible Hawaiian.

"She's very lovely . . . very vibrant and striking. I suppose Dillon has known her for a long time." Laine made the comment casually, surprising herself with the intentional probe.

"Long enough. But her bait has not yet lured the fish into the net." Miri gave a sly smile lost on the woman who stared into her milk. "You think Dillon looks good?"

"Looks good?" Laine repeated and frowned,

not understanding the nuance. "Yes, Dillon's a very attractive man. At least, I suppose he is; I haven't known many men."

"You should give him more smiles," Miri advised with a wise nod. "A smart woman uses smiles to show a man her mind."

"He hasn't given me many reasons to smile at him," Laine said between bites. "And," she continued, finding she resented the thought, "I would think he gets an abundance of smiles from other sources."

"Dillon gives his attention to many women. He is a generous man." Miri chuckled, and Laine blushed as she grasped the innuendo. "He has not yet found a woman who could make him selfish. Now you . . ." Miri tapped a finger aside her nose as if considering. "You would do well with him. He could teach you, and you could teach him."

"I teach Dillon?" Laine shook her head and gave a small laugh. "One cannot teach what one doesn't know. In the first place, Miri, I only met Dillon yesterday. All he's done so far is confuse me. From one moment to the next, I don't know how he's going to make me feel." She sighed, not realizing the sound was wistful. "I think men are very strange, Miri. I don't understand them at all."

"Understand?" Her bright laugh rattled through the kitchen. "What need is there to understand? You need only enjoy. I had three husbands, and I never understood one of them. But"—her smile was suddenly young—"I enjoyed. You are very young," she added. "That alone is attractive to a man used to women of knowledge."

"I don't think . . . I mean, of course, I wouldn't want him to, but . . ." Laine fumbled and stuttered, finding her thoughts a mass of confusion. "I'm sure Dillon wouldn't be interested in me. He seems to have a very compatible relationship with Miss King. Besides," Laine shrugged her shoulders as she felt depression growing, "he distrusts me."

"It is a stupid woman who lets what is gone interfere with what is now." Miri placed her fingertips together and leaned back in her chair. "You want your father's love, Skinny Bones? Time and patience will give it to you. You want Dillon?" She held up an imperial hand at Laine's automatic protest. "You will learn to fight as a woman fights." She stood, and the flowers on her muumuu trembled with the movement. "Now, out of my kitchen. I have much work to do."

Obediently, Laine rose and moved to the door. "Miri . . ." Nibbling her lips, she turned back. "You've been very close to my father for many years. Don't you . . ." Laine hesitated, then finished in a rush. "Don't you resent me just appearing like this after all these years?"

"Resent?" Miri repeated the word, then ran her tongue along the inside of her mouth. "I do not resent because resent is a waste of time. And the last thing I resent is a child." She picked up a large spoon and tapped it idly against her palm. "When you went away from Cap Simmons, you were a child and you went with your mother. Now, you are not a child, and you are here. What do I have to resent?" Miri shrugged and moved back to the stove.

Feeling unexpected tears, Laine shut her eyes on them and drew a small breath. "Thank you, Miri." With a murmur, she retreated to her room.

Thoughts swirled inside Laine's mind as she sat alone in her bedroom. As Dillon's embrace had opened a door to dormant emotions, so Miri's words had opened a door to dormant thoughts. *Time and patience*, Laine repeated silently. Time and patience were Miri's prescription for a daughter's troubled heart. But I have so little time, and little more patience. How can I win my father's love in a matter of days? She shook her head, unable to resolve an answer. *And Dillon*, her heart murmured as she threw herself onto the bed and stared at the ceiling. Why must he complicate an already impossibly complicated situation? Why must he embrace me, making me think and feel as a woman one moment, then push me away and stand as my accusor the next? He can be so gentle when you're in his arms, so warm. And then . . . Frustrated, she rolled over, laying her cheek against the pillow. Then he's so cold, and even his eyes are brutal. If only I could stop thinking of him, stop remembering how it feels to be kissed by him. It's only that I have no experience, and he has so much. It's nothing more than a physical awakening. There can be nothing more . . . nothing more.

The knock on Laine's door brought her up with a start. Pushing at her tousled hair, she rose to answer. Dillon had exchanged cut-offs for jeans, and he appeared as refreshed and alert as she did bemused and heavy-lidded. Laine stared at him dumbly, unable to bring her thoughts and words together. With a frown, he surveyed her sleep-flushed cheeks and soft eyes.

"Did I wake you?"

"No, I . . ." She glanced back at the clock, and her confusion grew as she noted that an hour had passed since she had first stretched out on the bed. "Yes," she amended. "I suppose the flight finally caught up with me." She reached up and ran a hand through her hair, struggling to orient herself. "I didn't even realize I'd been asleep."

"They're real, aren't they?"

"What?" Laine blinked and tried to sort out his meaning.

"The lashes." He was staring so intently into her eyes, Laine had to fight the need to look away.

Nonchalantly, he leaned against the door and completed his survey. "I'm on my way to the airport. I thought you might want to go. You said you wanted to see it again."

"Yes, I would." She was surprised by his courtesy.

"Well," he said dryly, and gestured for her to come along.

"Oh, I'll be right there. It should only take me a minute to get ready."

"You look ready."

"I need to comb my hair."

"It's fine." Dillon grabbed her hand and pulled her from the room before she could resist further.

Outside she found, to her astonishment, a helmet being thrust in her hands as she faced a shining, trim motorcycle. Clearing her throat, she looked from the helmet, to the machine, to Dillon. "We're going to ride on this?"

"That's right. I don't often use the car just to run to the airport."

"You might find this a good time to do so," Laine advised. "I've never ridden on a motorcycle."

"Duchess, all you have to do is to sit down and hang on." Dillon took the helmet from her and dropped it on her head. Securing his own helmet, he straddled the bike, then kicked the starter into life. "Climb on."

With amazement, Laine found herself astride the purring machine and clutching Dillon's waist as the motorcycle shot down the drive. Her death grip eased slightly as she realized that the speed was moderate, and the motorcycle had every intention of staying upright. It purred along the paved road.

Beside them, a river wandered like an unfurled blue ribbon, dividing patterned fields of taro. There was an excitement in being open to the wind, in feeling the hardness of Dillon's muscles beneath her hands. A sense of liberation flooded her. Laine realized that, in one day, Dillon had already given her experiences she might never have touched. I never knew how limited my life was, she thought with a smile. *No matter what happens, when I leave here, nothing will ever be quite the same again.*

When they arrived at the airport, Dillon wove through the main lot, circling to the back and halting in front of a hangar. "Off you go, Duchess. Ride's over."

Laine eased from the bike and struggled with her helmet. "Here." Dillon pulled it off for her, then dropped it to join his on the seat of the bike. "Still in one piece?"

"Actually," she returned, "I think I enjoyed it."

"It has its advantages." He ran his hands down her arms, then captured her waist. Laine stood very still, unwilling to retreat from his touch. He bent down and moved his mouth with teasing lightness over hers. Currents of pleasure ran over her skin. "Later," he said, pulling back. "I intend to finish that in a more satisfactory manner. But at the moment, I've work to do." His thumbs ran in lazy circles over her hips. "Cap's going to take you around; he's expecting you. Can you find your way?"

"Yes." Confused by the urgency of her heartbeat, Laine stepped back. The break in contact did nothing to slow it. "Am I to go to his office?"

"Yeah, the same place you went before. He'll show you whatever you want to see. Watch your step, Laine." His green eyes cooled abruptly, and his voice lost its lightness. "Until I'm sure about you, you can't afford to make any mistakes."

For a moment, she only stared up at him, feeling her skin grow cold, and her pulse slow. "I'm very much afraid," she admitted sadly, "I've already made one."

Turning, she walked away.

Chapter Six

Laine walked toward the small, palm-flanked building. Through her mind ran all which had passed in twenty-four hours. She had met her father, learned of her mother's deception and was now readjusting her wishes.

She had also, in the brief span of time it takes the sun to rise and fall, discovered the pleasures and demands of womanhood. Dillon had released new and magic sensations. Again, her mind argued with her heart that her feelings were only the result of a first physical attraction. It could hardly be anything else, she assured herself. One does not fall in love in a day, and certainly not with a man like Dillon O'Brian. We're total opposites. He's outgoing and confident, and so completely at ease with people. I envy him his honest confidence. There's nothing emotional about that. I've simply never met anyone like him before. That's why I'm confused. It has nothing to do with emotions. Laine felt comforted as she entered her father's office building.

As she stepped into the outer lobby, Cap strode from his office, glancing over his shoulder at a dark girl with a pad in her hand who was following in his wake.

"Check with Dillon on the fuel order before you send that out. He'll be in a meeting for the next hour. If you miss him at his office, try hangar four." As he caught sight of Laine, Cap smiled and slowed his pace. "Hello, Laine. Dillon said you wanted a tour."

"Yes, I'd love one, if you have the time."

"Of course. Sharon, this is my daughter. Laine, this is Sharon Kumocko, my secretary."

Laine observed the curiosity in Sharon's eyes as they exchanged greetings. Her father's tone during the introductions had been somewhat forced. Laine felt him hesitate before he took her arm to lead her outside. She wondered briefly if she had imagined their closeness during her childhood.

"It's not a very big airport," Cap began as they stepped out into the sun and heat. "For the most part, we cater to island hoppers and charters. We also run a flight school. That's essentially Dillon's project."

"Cap." Impulsively, Laine halted his recital

and turned to face him. "I know I've put you in an awkward position. I realize now that I should have written and asked if I could come rather than just dropping on your doorstep this way. It was thoughtless of me."

"Laine . . ."

"Please." She shook her head at his interruption and rushed on. "I realize, too, that you have your own life, your own home, your own friends. You've had fifteen years to settle into a routine. I don't want to interfere with any of that. Believe me, I don't want to be in the way, and I don't want you to feel . . ." She made a helpless gesture as the impetus ran out of her words. "I would like it if we could be friends."

Cap had studied her during her speech. The smile he gave her at its finish held more warmth than those he had given her before. "You know," he sighed, tugging his fingers through his hair, "it's sort of terrifying to be faced with a grown-up daughter. I missed all the stages, all the changes. I'm afraid I still pictured you as a bad-tempered pig-tailed urchin with scraped knees. The elegant woman who walked into my office yesterday and spoke to me with a faint French accent is a stranger. And one," he added, touching her hair a moment, "who brings back memories I thought I'd buried." He sighed again and stuck his hands in his pockets. "I don't know much about women; I don't think I ever did. Your mother was the most beautiful, confusing woman I've ever known. When you were little, and the three of us were still together, I substituted your friendship for the friendship that your mother and I never had. You were the only female I ever understood. I've always wondered if that was why things didn't work."

Tilting her head, Laine gave her father a long, searching look. "Cap, why did you marry her? There seems to be nothing you had in common."

Cap shook his head with a quick laugh. "You didn't know her twenty years ago. She did a lot of changing, Laine. Some people change more than others." He shook his head again, and his eyes focused on some middle distance. "Besides, I loved her. I've always loved her."

"I'm sorry." Laine felt tears burn the back of her eyes, and she dropped her gaze to the ground. "I don't mean to make things more difficult."

"You're not. We had some good years." He paused until Laine lifted her eyes. "I like to remember them now and again." Taking her arm, he began to walk. "Was your mother happy, Laine?"

"Happy?" She thought a moment, remembering the quicksilver moods, the gay bubbling voice with dissatisfaction always under the surface. "I suppose Vanessa was as happy as she was capable of being. She loved Paris and she lived as she chose."

"Vanessa?" Cap frowned, glancing down at Laine's profile. "Is that how you think of your mother?"

"I always called her by name." Laine lifted her hand to shield her eyes from the sun as she watched the descent of a charter. "She said 'mother' made her feel too old. She hated getting older. . . . I feel better knowing you're happy in the life you've chosen. Do you fly anymore, Cap? I remember how you used to love it."

"I still put in my quota of flight hours. Laine," he took both her arms and turned her to face him, "one question, then we'll leave it alone for a while. Have you been happy?"

The directness of both his question and his eyes caused her to fumble. She looked away as if fascinated by disembarking passengers. "I've been very busy. The nuns are very serious about education."

"You're not answering my question. Or," he corrected, drawing his thick brows together, "maybe you are."

"I've been content," she said, giving him a smile. "I've learned a great deal, and I'm comfortable with my life. I think that's enough for anyone."

"For someone," Cap returned, "who's reached my age, but not for a very young, very lovely woman." He watched her smile fade into perplexity. "It's not enough, Laine, and I'm surprised you'd settle for it." His voice was stern, laced with a hint of disapproval which put Laine on the defensive.

"Cap, I haven't had the chance . . ." She stopped, realizing she must guard her words. "I haven't taken the time," she amended, "to chase windmills." She lifted her hands, palms up, in a broad French gesture. "Perhaps I've reached the point in my life when I should begin to do so."

His expression lightened as she smiled up at him. "All right, we'll let it rest for now."

Without any more mention of the past, Cap led Laine through neat rows of planes. He fondled each as if it were a child, explaining their qualities in proud, but to Laine hopelessly technical, terms. She listened, content with his good humor, pleased with the sound of his voice. Occasionally, she made an ignorant comment that made him laugh. She found the laugh very precious.

The buildings were spread out, neat and without pretension; hangars and storage buildings, research and accounting offices, with the high, glass-enclosed control tower dominating all. Cap pointed out each one, but the planes themselves were his consummate interest.

"You said it wasn't big." Laine gazed around the complex and down light-dotted runways. "It looks enormous."

"It's a small, low activity field, but we do our best to see that it's as well run as Honolulu International."

"What is it that Dillon does here?" Telling herself it was only idle curiosity, Laine surrendered to the urge to question.

"Oh, Dillon does a bit of everything," Cap answered with frustrating vagueness. "He has a knack for organizing. He can find his way through a problem before it becomes one, and he handles people so well they never realize they've been handled. He can also take a plane apart and put it back together again." Smiling, Cap gave a small shake of his head. "I don't know what I'd have done without Dillon. Without his drive, I might have been content to be a crop duster."

"Drive?" Laine repeated, lingering over the word. "Yes, I suppose he has drive when there is something he wants. But isn't he . . ." She searched for a label and settled on a generality. "Isn't he a very casual person?"

"Island life breeds a certain casualness, Laine, and Dillon was born here." He steered her toward the communications building. "Just because a man is at ease with himself and avoids pretension doesn't mean he lacks intelligence or ability. Dillon has both; he simply pursues his ambitions in his own way."

Later, as they walked toward the steel-domed hangars, Laine realized she and her father had begun to build a new relationship. He was more relaxed with her, his smiles and speech more spontaneous. She knew her shield was dropped as well, and she was more vulnerable.

"I've an appointment in a few minutes." Cap stopped just inside the building and glanced at his watch. "I'll have to turn you over to Dillon now, unless you want me to have someone take you back to the house."

"No, I'll be fine," she assured him. "Perhaps I can just wander about. I don't want to be a nuisance."

"You haven't been a nuisance. I enjoyed taking you through. You haven't lost the curiosity I remember. You always wanted to know why and how and you always listened. I think you were five when you demanded I explain the entire control panel of a 707." His chuckle was the same quick, appealing sound she remembered from childhood. "Your face would get so serious, I'd swear you had understood everything I'd said." He patted her hand, then smiled over her head. "Dillon, I thought we'd find you here. Take care of Laine, will you? I've got Billet coming in."

"It appears I've got the best of the deal."

Laine turned to see him leaning against a plane, wiping his hand on the loose coveralls he wore.

"Did everything go all right with the union representative?"

"Fine. You can look over the report tomorrow."

"I'll see you tonight, then." Cap turned to

Laine, and after a brief hesitation, patted her cheek before he walked away.

Smiling, she turned back to encounter Dillon's brooding stare. "Oh, please," she began, shaking her head. "Don't spoil it. It's such a small thing."

With a shrug, Dillon turned back to the plane. "Did you like your tour?"

"Yes, I did." Laine's footsteps echoed off the high ceiling as she crossed the room to join him. "I'm afraid I didn't understand a fraction of what he told me. He carried on about aprons and funnel systems and became very expansive on wind drag and thrust." She creased her brow for a moment as she searched her memory. "I'm told struts can withstand comprehensive as well as tensile forces. I didn't have the courage to confess I didn't know one force from the other."

"He's happiest when he's talking about planes," Dillon commented absently. "It doesn't matter if you understood as long as you listened. Hand me that torque wrench."

Laine looked down at the assortment of tools, then searched for something resembling a torque wrench. "I enjoyed listening. Is this a wrench?"

Dillon twisted his head and glanced at the ratchet she offered. With reluctant amusement, he brought his eyes to hers, then shook his head. "No, Duchess. This," he stated, finding the tool himself, "is a wrench."

"I haven't spent a great deal of time under

cars or under planes," she muttered. Her annoyance spread as she thought how unlikely it was that he would ask Orchid King for a torque wrench. "Cap told me you've added a flight school. Do you do the instructing?"

"Some."

Pumping up her courage, Laine asked in a rush, "Would you teach me?"

"What?" Dillon glanced back over his shoulder.

"Could you teach me to fly a plane?" She wondered if the question sounded as ridiculous to Dillon as it did to her.

"Maybe." He studied the fragile planes of her face, noting the determined light in her eyes. "Maybe," he repeated. "Why do you want to learn?"

"Cap used to talk about teaching me. Of course"—she spread her hands in a Gallic gesture—"I was only a child, but . . ." Releasing an impatient breath, Laine lifted her chin and was suddenly very American. "Because I think it would be fun."

The change, and the stubborn set to her mouth, touched off Dillon's laughter. "I'll take one of you up tomorrow." Laine frowned, trying to puzzle out his meaning. Turning back to the plane, Dillon held out the wrench for her to put away. She stared at the grease-smeared handle. Taking his head from the bowels of the plane, Dillon turned back and saw her reluctance. He muttered something she did not attempt to translate, then moved away and pulled another pair of coveralls from a hook. "Here, put these on. I'm going to be a while, and you might as well be useful."

"I'm sure you'd manage beautifully without me."

"Undoubtedly, but put them on anyway." Under Dillon's watchful eye, Laine stepped into the coveralls and slipped her arms into the sleeves. "Good grief, you look swallowed." Crouching down, he began to roll up the pants legs while she scowled at the top of his head."

"I'm sure you'll find me more hindrance than help."

"I figured that out some time ago," he replied. His tone was undeniably cheerful as he rolled up her sleeves half a dozen times. "You shouldn't have quit growing so soon; you don't look more than twelve." He pulled the zipper up to her throat in one swift motion, then looked into her face. She saw his expression alter. For an instant, she thought she observed a flash of tenderness before he let out an impatient breath. Cursing softly, he submerged into the belly of the plane. "All right," he began briskly, "hand me a screwdriver. The one with the red handle."

Having made the acquaintance of this particular tool, Laine foraged and found it. She placed it in Dillon's outstretched hand. He worked for some time, his conversation limited almost exclusively to the request and description of tools. As time passed, the hum of planes outside became only a backdrop for his voice.

Laine began to ask him questions about the job he was performing. She felt no need to follow his answers, finding pleasure only in the tone and texture of his voice. He was absorbed and she was able to study him unobserved. She surveyed the odd intensity of his eyes, the firm line of his chin and jaw, the bronzed skin which rippled along his arm as he worked. She saw that his chin was shadowed with a day-old beard, that his hair was curling loosely over his collar, that his right brow was lifted slightly higher than his left as he concentrated.

Dillon turned to her with some request, but she could only stare. She was lost in his eyes, blanketed by a fierce and trembling realization.

"What's wrong?" Dillon drew his brows together.

Like a diver breaking water, Laine shook her head and swallowed. "Nothing, I . . . What did you want? I wasn't paying attention." She bent over the box of tools as if it contained the focus of her world. Silently, Dillon lifted out the one he required and turned back to the engine. Grateful for his preoccupation, Laine closed her eyes. She felt bemused and defenseless.

Love, she thought, *should not come with such quick intensity. It should flow slowly, with tenderness and gentle feelings. It shouldn't stab like a sword, striking without warning, without mercy. How could one love what one could not understand?* Dillon O'Brian was an enigma, a man whose moods seemed to flow without rhyme or reason. And what did she know of him? He was her father's partner, but his position was unclear. He was a man who knew both the sky and the sea, and found it easy to move with their freedom. She knew too that he was a man who knew women and could give them pleasure.

And how, Laine wondered, does one fight love when one has no knowledge of it? Perhaps it was a matter of balance. She deliberately released the tension in her shoulders. I have to find the way to walk the wire without leaning over either side and tumbling off.

"It seems you've taken a side trip," Dillon commented, pulling a rag from his pocket. He grinned as Laine gave a start of alarm. "You're a miserable mechanic, Duchess, and a sloppy one." He rubbed the rag over her cheek until a black smudge disappeared. "There's a sink over there; you'd better go wash your hands. I'll finish these adjustments later. The fuel system is giving me fits."

Laine moved off as he instructed, taking her time in removing traces of grime. She used the opportunity to regain her composure. Hanging up the borrowed overalls, she wandered about the empty hangar while Dillon packed away tools and completed his own washing up. She was surprised to see that it had grown late during the time she had inexpertly assisted Dillon. A soft dusk masked the day's brilliance. Along the runways, lights twinkled like small red eyes. As she turned back, Laine found Dillon's gaze on her. She moistened her lips, then attempted casualness.

"Are you finished?"

"Not quite. Come here." Something in his tone caused her to retreat a step rather than obey. He lifted his brows, then repeated the order with a soft, underlying threat. "I said come here."

Deciding voluntary agreement was the wisest choice, Laine crossed the floor. Her echoing footsteps seemed to bounce off the walls like thunder. She prayed the sound masked the furious booming of her heart as she stopped in front of him, and that its beating was in her ears only. She stood in silence as he studied her face, wishing desperately she knew what he was looking for, and if she possessed it. Dillon said nothing, but placed his hands on her hips, drawing her a step closer. Their thighs brushed. His grip was firm, and all the while his eyes kept hers a prisoner.

"Kiss me," he said simply. She shook her head in quick protest, unable to look or break away. "Laine, I said kiss me." Dillon pressed her hips closer, molding her shape to his. His eyes were demanding, his mouth tempting. Tentatively, she lifted her arms, letting her hands rest on his shoulders as she rose to her toes. Her eyes remained open and locked on his as their faces drew nearer, as their breaths began to mingle. Softly, she touched her lips to his.

He waited until her mouth lost its shyness and became mobile on his, waited until her arms found their way around his neck to urge him closer. He increased the pressure, drawing out her sigh as he slid his hands under her blouse to the smooth skin of her back. His explorations were slow and achingly gentle. The hands that caressed her taught rather than demanded. Murmuring his name against the taste of his mouth, Laine strained against him, wanting him, needing him. The swift heat of passion was all consuming. Her lips seemed to learn more quickly than her brain. They began to seek and demand pleasures she could not yet understand. The rest of the world faded like a whisper. At that moment, there was nothing in her life but Dillon and her need for him.

He drew her away. Neither spoke, each staring into the other's eyes as if to read a message not yet written. Dillon brushed a stray curl from her cheek. "I'd better take you home."

"Dillon," Laine began, completely at a loss as to what could be said. Unable to continue, she closed her eyes on her own inadequacy.

"Come on, Duchess, you've had a long day." Dillon circled her neck with his hand and massaged briefly. "We're not dealing on equal footing at the moment, and I like to fight fair under most circumstances."

"Fight?" Laine managed, struggling to keep her eyes open and steady on his. "Is that what this is, Dillon? A fight?"

"The oldest kind," he returned with a small lift to his mouth. His smile faded before it was truly formed, and suddenly his hand was firm on her chin. "It's not over, Laine, and when we have the next round, I might say the devil with the rules."

Chapter Seven

When Laine came down for breakfast the next morning, she found only her father. "Hello, Skinny Bones," Miri called out before Cap could greet her. "Sit and eat. I will fix you tea since you do not like my coffee."

Unsure whether to be embarrassed or amused, Laine obeyed. "Thank you, Miri," she said to the retreating back.

"She's quite taken with you." Looking over, Laine saw the light of mirth in Cap's eyes. "Since you've come, she's been so wrapped up with putting pounds on you, she hasn't made one comment about me needing a wife."

With a wry smile, Laine watched her father pour his coffee. "Glad to help. I showed myself around a bit yesterday. I hope you don't mind."

"No, of course not." His smile was rueful. "I guess I should've taken you around the house myself. My manners are a little rusty."

"I didn't mind. Actually," she tilted her head and returned his smile, "wandering around alone gave me a sort of fresh perspective. You said you'd missed all the stages and still thought of me as a child. I think . . ." Her fingers spread as she tried to clarify her thoughts. "I think I missed them too—that is, I still had my childhood image of you. Yesterday, I began to see James Simmons in flesh and blood."

"Disappointed?" There was more ease in his tone and a lurking humor in his eyes.

"Impressed," Laine corrected. "I saw a man content with himself and his life, who has the love and respect of those close to him. I think my father must be a very nice man."

He gave her an odd smile which spoke both of surprise and pleasure. "That's quite a compliment coming from a grown daughter." He added more coffee to his cup, and Laine let the silence drift. Her gaze lingered on Dillon's empty seat a moment. "Ah . . . Is Dillon not here?"

"Hmm? Oh, Dillon had a breakfast meeting. As a matter of fact, he has quite a few things to see to this morning." Cap drank his coffee black, and with an enjoyment Laine could not understand.

"I see," she responded, trying not to sound

disappointed. "I suppose the airport keeps both of you very busy."

"That it does." Cap glanced at his watch and tilted his head in regret. "Actually, I have an appointment myself very shortly. I'm sorry to leave you alone this way, but . . ."

"Please," Laine interrupted. "I don't need to be entertained, and I meant what I said yesterday about not wanting to interfere. I'm sure I'll find plenty of things to keep me occupied."

"All right then. I'll see you this evening." Cap rose, then paused at the doorway with sudden inspiration. "Miri can arrange a ride for you if you'd like to do some shopping in town."

"Thank you." Laine smiled, thinking of her limited funds. "Perhaps I will." She watched him stroll away, then sighed as her gaze fell again on Dillon's empty chair.

Laine's morning was spent lazily. She soon found out that Miri would not accept or tolerate any help around the house. Following the native woman's strong suggestion that she go out, Laine gathered her stationery and set out for the bay. She found it every bit as perfect as she had the day before—the water clear as crystal, the sand white and pure. Spreading out a blanket, Laine sat down and tried to describe her surroundings with words on paper. The letters she wrote to France were long and detailed, though she omitted any mention of her troubled situation.

As she wrote, the sun rose high overhead. The air was moist and ripe. Lulled by the peace and the rays of the sun, she curled up on the blanket and slept.

Her limbs were languid, and behind closed lids was a dull red mist. She wondered hazily how the Reverend Mother had urged so much heat out of the ancient furnace. Reluctantly, she struggled to toss off sleep as a hand shook her shoulder. *"Un moment, ma soeur,"* she murmured, and sighed with the effort. *"J'arrive."* Forcing open her leaden lids, she found Dillon's face inches above hers.

"I seem to have a habit of waking you up." He leaned back on his heels and studied her cloudy eyes. "Don't you know better than to sleep in the sun with that complexion? You're lucky you didn't burn."

"Oh." At last realizing where she was, Laine pushed herself into a sitting position. She felt the odd sense of guilt of the napper caught napping. "I don't know why I fell asleep like that. It must have been the quiet."

"Another reason might be exhaustion," Dillon countered, then frowned. "You're losing the shadows under your eyes."

"Cap said you were very busy this morning." Laine found his continued survey disconcerting and shuffled her writing gear.

"Hmm, yes, I was. Writing letters?"

She glanced up at him, then tapped the tip of her pen against her mouth. "Hmm, yes, I was."

"Very cute." His mouth twitched slightly as he hauled her to her feet. "I thought you wanted to learn how to fly a plane."

"Oh!" Her face lit up with pleasure. "I thought you'd forgotten. Are you sure you're not too busy? Cap said . . ."

"No, I hadn't forgotten, and no, I'm not too busy." He cut her off as he leaned down to gather her blanket. "Stop babbling as if you were twelve and I were taking you to the circus for cotton candy."

"Of course," she replied, amused by his reaction.

Dillon let out an exasperated breath before grabbing her hand and pulling her across the sand. She heard him mutter something uncomplimentary about women in general.

Less than an hour later, Laine found herself seated in Dillon's plane. "Now, this is a single prop monoplane with a reciprocating engine. Another time, I'll take you up in the jet, but . . ."

"You have another plane?" Laine interrupted.

"Some people collect hats," Dillon countered dryly, then pointed to the variety of gauges. "Basically, flying a plane is no more difficult than driving a car. The first thing you have to do is understand your instruments and learn how to read them."

"There are quite a few, aren't there?" Dubiously, Laine scanned numbers and needles.

"Not really. This isn't exactly an X-15." He

let out a long breath at her blank expression, then started the engine. "O.K., as we climb, I want you to watch this gauge. It's the altimeter. It . . ."

"It indicates the height of the plane above sea level or above ground," Laine finished for him.

"Very good." Dillon cleared his takeoff with the tower, and the plane began its roll down the runway. "What did you do, grab one of Cap's magazines last night?"

"No. I remember some of my early lessons. I suppose I stored away all the things Cap used to ramble about when I was a child. This is a compass, and this . . ." Her brow furrowed in her memory search. "This is a turn and bank indicator, but I'm not sure I remember quite what that means."

"I'm impressed, but you're supposed to be watching the altimeter."

"Oh, yes." Wrinkling her nose at the chastisement, she obeyed.

"All right." Dillon gave her profile a quick grin, then turned his attention to the sky. "The larger needle's going to make one turn of the dial for every thousand feet we climb. The smaller one makes a turn for every ten thousand. Once you learn your gauges, and how to use each one of them, your job's less difficult than driving, and there's generally a lot less traffic."

"Perhaps you'll teach me to drive a car next," Laine suggested as she watched the large needle round the dial for the second time.

"You don't know how to drive?" Dillon demanded. His voice was incredulous.

"No. Is that a crime in this country? I assure you, there are some people who believe me to be marginally intelligent. I'm certain I can learn to fly this machine in the same amount of time it takes any of your other students."

"It's possible," Dillon muttered. "How come you never learned to drive a car?"

"Because I never had one. How did you break your nose?" At his puzzled expression, Laine merely gave him a bland smile. "My question is just as irrelevant as yours."

Laine felt quite pleased when he laughed, almost as though she had won a small victory.

"Which time?" he asked, and it was her turn to look puzzled. "I broke it twice. The first time I was about ten and tried to fly a cardboard plane I had designed off the roof of the garage. I didn't have the propulsion system perfected. I only broke my nose and my arm, though I was told it should've been my neck."

"Very likely," Laine agreed. "And the second time?"

"The second time, I was a bit older. There was a disagreement over a certain girl. My nose suffered another insult, and the other guy lost two teeth."

"Older perhaps, but little wiser," Laine commented. "And who got the girl?"

Dillon flashed his quick grin. "Neither of us. We decided she wasn't worth it after all and went off to nurse our wounds with a beer."

"How gallant."

"Yeah, I'm sure you've noticed that trait in me. I can't seem to shake it. Now, watch your famous turn and bank indicator, and I'll explain its function."

For the next thirty minutes, he became the quintessential teacher, surprising Laine with his knowledge and patience. He answered the dozens of questions she tossed out as flashes of her early lessons skipped through her memory. He seemed to accept her sudden thirst to know as if it were not only natural, but expected. They cruised through a sky touched with puffy clouds and mountain peaks and skimmed the gaping mouth of the multihued Waimea Canyon. They circled above the endless, white-capped ocean. Laine began to see the similarity between the freedom of the sky and the freedom of the sea. She began to feel the fascination Dillon had spoken of, the need to meet the challenge, the need to explore. She listened with every ounce of her concentration, determined to understand and remember.

"There's a little storm behind us," Dillon announced casually. "We're not going to beat it back." He turned to Laine with a faint smile on his lips. "We're going to get tossed around a bit, Duchess."

"Oh?" Trying to mirror his mood, Laine shifted in her seat and studied the dark clouds in their wake. "Can you fly through that?" she asked, keeping her voice light while her stomach tightened.

"Oh, maybe," he returned. She jerked her head around swiftly. When she saw the laughter in his eyes, she let out a long breath.

"You have an odd sense of humor, Dillon. Very unique," she added, then sucked in her breath as the clouds overtook them. All at once, they were shrouded in darkness, rain pelting furiously on all sides. As the plane rocked, Laine felt a surge of panic.

"You know, it always fascinates me to be in a cloud. Nothing much to them, just vapor and moisture, but they're fabulous." His voice was calm and composed. Laine felt her heartbeat steadying. "Storm clouds are the most interesting, but you really need lightning."

"I think I could live without it," Laine murmured.

"That's because you haven't seen it from up here. When you fly above lightning, you can watch it kicking up inside the clouds. The colors are incredible."

"Have you flown through many storms?" Laine looked out her window, but saw nothing but swirling black clouds.

"I've done my share. The front of this one'll

be waiting for us when we land. Won't last long though." The plane bucked again, and Laine looked on in bewilderment as Dillon grinned.

"You enjoy this sort of thing, don't you? The excitement, the sense of danger?"

"It keeps the reflexes in tune, Laine." Turning, he smiled at her without a trace of cynicism. "And it keeps life from being boring." The look held for a moment, and Laine's heart did a series of jumping jacks. "There's plenty of stability in life," he continued, making adjustments to compensate for the wind. "Jobs, bills, insurance policies, that's what gives you balance. But sometimes, you've got to ride a roller coaster, run a race, ride a wave. That's what makes life fun. The trick is to keep one end of the scope from overbalancing the other."

Yes, Laine thought. Vanessa never learned the trick. She was always looking for a new game and never enjoyed the one she was playing. And perhaps I've overcompensated by thinking too much of the stability. Too many books, and not enough doing. Laine felt her muscles relax and she turned to Dillon with a hint of a smile. "I haven't ridden a roller coaster for a great many years. One could say that I'm due. Look!" She pressed her face against the side window and peered downward. "It's like something out of Macbeth, all misty and sinister. I'd like to see the lightning, Dillon. I really would."

He laughed at the eager anticipation on her face as he began his descent. "I'll see if I can arrange it."

The clouds seemed to swirl and dissolve as the plane lost altitude. Their thickness became pale gray cobwebs to be dusted out of the way. Below, the landscape came into view as they dropped below the mist. The earth was rain-drenched and vivid with color. As they landed, Laine felt her pleasure fade into a vague sense of loss. She felt like a child who has just blown out her last birthday candle.

"I'll take you back up in a couple days if you want," said Dillon, taxiing to a halt.

"Yes, please, I'd like that very much. I don't know how to thank you for . . ."

"Do your homework," he said as he shut off the engine. "I'll give you some books and you can read up on instrumentation."

"Yes, sir," Laine said with suspicious humility. Dillon glared at her briefly before swinging from the plane. Laine's lack of experience caused her to take more time with her exit. She found herself swooped down before she could complete the journey on her own.

In the pounding rain they stood close, Dillon's hands light on her waist. She could feel the heat of his body through the dampness of her blouse. Dark tendrils of hair fell over his forehead, and without thought, Laine lifted her hand to smooth them back. There was something sweetly ordinary about being in his arms, as if it were a place she had been countless times before and would come back to countless times again. She felt her love bursting to be free.

"You're getting wet," she murmured, dropping her hand to his cheek.

"So are you." Though his fingers tightened on her waist, he drew her no closer.

"I don't mind."

With a sigh, Dillon rested his chin on the top of her head. "Miri'll punch out on me if I let you catch a chill."

"I'm not cold," she murmured, finding indescribable pleasure in their closeness.

"You're shivering." Abruptly, Dillon brought her to his side and began to walk. "We'll go into my office, and you can dry out before I take you home."

As they walked, the rain slowed to a mist. Fingers of sunlight began to strain through, brushing away the last stubborn drops. Laine surveyed the complex. She remembered the building which housed Dillon's office from the tour she had taken with her father. With a grin, she pushed damp hair from her eyes and pulled away from Dillon. "Race you," she challenged, and scrambled over wet pavement.

He caught her, laughing and breathless, at the door. With a new ease, Laine circled his neck as they laughed together. She felt young and foolish and desperately in love.

"You're quick, aren't you?" Dillon observed, and she tilted her head back to meet his smile.

"You learn to be quick when you live in a dormitory. Competition for the bath is brutal." Laine thought she saw his smile begin to fade before they were interrupted.

"Dillon, I'm sorry to disturb you."

Glancing over, Laine saw a young woman with classic bone structure, her raven hair pulled taut at the nape of a slender neck. The woman returned Laine's survey with undisguised curiosity. Blushing, Laine struggled out of Dillon's arms.

"It's all right, Fran. This is Laine Simmons, Cap's daughter. Fran's my calculator."

"He means secretary," Fran returned with an exasperated sigh. "But this afternoon I feel more like an answering service. You have a dozen phone messages on your desk."

"Anything urgent?" As he asked, he moved into an adjoining room.

"No." Fran gave Laine a friendly smile. "Just several people who didn't want to make a decision until they heard from Mount Olympus. I told them all you were out for the day and would get back to them tomorrow."

"Good." Walking back into the room, Dillon carried a handful of papers and a towel. He tossed the towel at Laine before he studied the papers.

"I thought you were supposed to be taking a few days off," Fran stated while Dillon muttered over his messages.

"Um-hum. There doesn't seem to be anything here that can't wait."

"I've already told you that." Fran snatched the papers out of his hand.

"So you did." Unabashed, Dillon grinned and patted her cheek. "Did you ask Orchid what she wanted?"

Across the room, Laine stopped rubbing the towel against her hair, then began again with increased speed.

"No, though after the *third* call, I'm afraid I became a bit abrupt with her."

"She can handle it," Dillon returned easily, then switched his attention to Laine. "Ready?"

"Yes." Feeling curiously deflated, Laine crossed the room and handed Dillon the towel. "Thank you."

"Sure." Casually, he tossed the damp towel to Fran. "See you tomorrow, cousin."

"Yes, master." Fran shot Laine a friendly wave before Dillon hustled her from the building.

With a great deal of effort, Laine managed to thrust Orchid King from her mind during the drive home and throughout the evening meal. The sun was just setting when she settled on the porch with Dillon and her father.

The sky's light was enchanting. The intense, tropical blue was breaking into hues of gold and crimson, the low, misted clouds streaked with pinks and mauves. There was something dreamlike and soothing in the dusk. Laine sat quietly in a wicker chair, thinking over her day as the men's conversation washed over her. Even had she understood their exchange, she was too lazily content to join in. She knew that for the first time in her adult life, she was both physically and mentally relaxed. Perhaps, she mused, it was the adventures of the past few days, the testing of so many untried feelings and emotions.

Mumbling about coffee, Cap rose and slipped inside the house. Laine gave him an absent smile as he passed her, then curled her legs under her and watched the first stars blink into life.

"You're quiet tonight." As Dillon leaned back in his chair, Laine heard the soft click of his lighter.

"I was just thinking how lovely it is here." Her sigh drifted with contentment. "I think it must be the loveliest place on earth."

"Lovelier than Paris?"

Hearing the edge in his voice, Laine turned to look at him questioningly. The first light of the moon fell gently over her face. "It's very different from Paris," she answered. "Parts of Paris are beautiful, mellowed and gentled with age. Other parts are elegant or dignified. She is like a woman who has been often told she is enchanting. But the beauty here is more primitive. The island is ageless and innocent at the same time.

"Many people tire of innocence." Dillon shrugged and drew deeply on his cigarette.

"I suppose that's true," she agreed, unsure why he seemed so distant and so cynical.

"In this light, you look a great deal like your mother," he said suddenly, and Laine felt her skin ice over.

"How do you know? You never met my mother."

"Cap has a picture." Dillon turned toward her, but his face was in shadows. "You resemble her a great deal."

"She certainly does." Cap sauntered out with a tray of coffee in his hands. Setting it on a round glass table, he straightened and studied Laine. "It's amazing. The light will catch you a certain way, or you'll get a certain expression on your face. Suddenly, it's your mother twenty years ago."

"I'm not Vanessa." Laine sprang up from her seat, and her voice trembled with rage. "I'm nothing like Vanessa." To her distress, tears began to gather in her eyes. Her father looked on in astonishment. "I'm nothing like her. I won't be compared to her." Furious with both the men and herself, Laine turned and slammed through the screen door. On her dash for the stairs, she collided with Miri's substantial form. Stuttering an apology, she streaked up the stairs and into her room.

Laine was pacing around her room for the third time when Miri strolled in.

"What is all this running and slamming in

my house?" Miri asked, folding her arms across her ample chest.

Shaking her head, Laine lowered herself to the bed, then despising herself, burst into tears. Clucking her tongue and muttering in Hawaiian, Miri crossed the room. Soon Laine found her head cradled against a soft, pillowing bosom. "That Dillon," Miri muttered as she rocked Laine to and fro.

"It wasn't Dillon," Laine managed, finding the maternal comfort new and overwhelming. "Yes, it was . . . it was both of them." Laine had a sudden desperate need for reassurance. "I'm nothing like her, Miri. I'm nothing like her at all."

"Of course you are not." Miri patted Laine's blond curls. "Who is it you are not like?"

"Vanessa." Laine brushed away tears with the back of her hand. "My mother. Both of them were looking at me, saying how much I look like her."

"What is this? What is this? All these tears because you look like someone?" Miri pulled Laine away by the shoulders and shook her. "Why do you waste your tears on this? I think you're a smart girl, then you act stupid."

"You don't understand." Laine drew up her knees and rested her chin on them. "I won't be compared to her, not to her. Vanessa was selfish and self-centered and dishonest."

"She was your mother," Miri stated with such authority that Laine's mouth dropped open. "You will speak with respect of your mother. She is dead, and whatever she did is over now. You must bury it," Miri commanded, giving Laine another shake, "or you will never be happy. Did they say you were selfish and self-centered and dishonest?"

"No, but . . ."

"What did Cap Simmons say to you?" Miri demanded.

Laine let out a long breath. "He said I looked like my mother."

"And do you, or does he lie?"

"Yes, I suppose I do, but . . ."

"So, your mother was a pretty woman, you are a pretty woman." Miri lifted Laine's chin with her thick fingers. "Do you know who you are, Laine Simmons?"

"Yes, I think I do."

"Then you have no problem." Miri patted her cheek and rose.

"Oh, Miri." Laine laughed and wiped her eyes again. "You make me feel very foolish."

"You make yourself feel foolish," Miri corrected. "I did not slam doors."

Laine sighed over Miri's logic. "I suppose I'll have to go down and apologize."

As Laine stood, Miri folded her arms and blocked her way. "You will do no such thing."

Staring at her, Laine let out a frustrated breath. "But you just said . . ."

"I said you were stupid, and you were. Cap Simmons and Dillon were also stupid. No woman should be compared to another woman. You are special, you are unique.

Sometimes men see only the face." Miri tapped a finger against each of her cheeks. "It takes them longer to see what is inside. So," she gave Laine a white-toothed smile, "you will not apologize, you will let them apologize. It is the best way."

"I see," Laine said, not seeing at all. Suddenly, she laughed and sat back on the bed. "Thank you, Miri, I feel much better."

"Good. Now go to bed. I will go lecture Cap Simmons and Dillon." There was an unmistakable note of anticipation in her voice.

Chapter Eight

The following morning Laine descended the stairs, her Nile-green sundress floating around her, leaving her arms and shoulders bare. Feeling awkward after the previous evening's incident, Laine paused at the doorway of the dining room. Her father and Dillon were already at breakfast and deep in discussion.

"If Bob needs next week off, I can easily take his shift on the charters." Dillon poured coffee as he spoke.

"You've got enough to do at your own place without taking that on too. Whatever happened to those few days off you were going to take?" Cap accepted the coffee and gave Dillon a stern look.

"I haven't exactly been chained to my desk the past week." Dillon grinned, then shrugged as Cap's expression remained unchanged. "I'll take some time off next month."

"Where have I heard that before?" Cap asked the ceiling. Dillon's grin flashed again.

"I didn't tell you I was retiring next year, did I?" Dillon sipped coffee casually, but Laine recognized the mischief in his voice. "I'm going to take up hang gliding while you slave away behind a desk. Who are you going to nag if I'm not around every day?"

"When you can stay away for more than a week at a time," Cap countered, "that's when *I'm* going to retire. The trouble with you," he wagged a spoon at Dillon in admonishment, "is that your mind's too good and you've let too many people find it out. Now you're stuck because nobody wants to make a move without checking with you first. You should've kept that aeronautical-engineering degree a secret. Hang gliding." Cap chuckled and lifted his cup. "Oh, hello, Laine."

Laine jolted at the sound of her name. "Good morning," she replied, hoping that her outburst the evening before had not cost her the slight progress she had made with her father.

"Is it safe to ask you in?" His smile was sheepish, but he beckoned her forward. "As I recall, your explosions were frequent, fierce, but short-lived."

Relieved he had not offered her a stilted apology, Laine took her place at the table. "Your memory is accurate, though I assure you, I explode at very infrequent intervals these days." She offered Dillon a tentative smile, determined to treat the matter lightly. "Good morning, Dillon."

"Morning, Duchess. Coffee?" Before she could refuse, he was filling her cup.

"Thank you," she murmured. "It's hard to believe, but I think today is more beautiful than yesterday. I don't believe I'd ever grow used to living in Paradise."

"You've barely seen any of it yet," Cap commented. "You should go up to the mountains, or to the center. You know, the center of Kauai is one of the wettest spots in the world. The rain forest is something to see."

"The island seems to have a lot of variety." Laine toyed with her coffee. "I can't imagine any of it is more beautiful than right here."

"I'll take you around a bit today," Dillon announced. Laine glanced sharply at him.

"I don't want to interfere with your routine. I've already taken up a great deal of your time." Laine had not yet regained her balance with Dillon. Her eyes were both wary and unsure.

"I've a bit more to spare." He rose abruptly. "I'll have things cleared up and be back around eleven. See you later, Cap." He strode out without waiting for her assent.

Miri entered with a full plate and placed it

in front of Laine. She scowled at the coffee. "Why do you pour coffee when you aren't going to drink it?" With a regal sniff, she picked up the cup and swooped from the room. With a sigh, Laine attacked her breakfast and wondered how the day would pass. She was to find the morning passed quickly.

As if granting a royal decree, Miri agreed to allow Laine to refresh the vases of flowers which were scattered throughout the house. Laine spent her morning hours in the garden. It was not a garden as Laine remembered from her early American years or from her later French ones. It was a spreading, sprawling, wild tangle of greens and tempestuous hues. The plants would not be organized or dictated to by plot or plan.

Inside again, Laine took special care in the arranging of the vases. Her mind drifted to the daffodils which would be blooming outside her window at school. She found it odd that she felt no trace of homesickness, no longing for the soft French voices of the sisters or the high, eager ones of her students. She knew that she was dangerously close to thinking of Kauai as home. The thought of returning to France and the life she led there filled her with a cold, dull ache.

In her father's den, Laine placed the vase of frangipani on his desk and glanced at the photograph of Cap and Dillon. *How strange*, she thought, *that I should need both of them so badly*. With a sigh, she buried her face in the blossoms.

"Do flowers make you unhappy?"

She whirled, nearly upsetting the vase. For a moment, she and Dillon stared at each other without speaking. Laine felt the tension between them, though its cause and meaning were unclear to her. "Hello. Is it eleven already?"

"It's nearly noon. I'm late." Dillon thrust his hands in his pockets and watched her. Behind her, the sun poured through the window to halo her hair. "Do you want some lunch?"

"No thank you," she said with conviction. She saw his eyes smile briefly.

"Are you ready?"

"Yes, I'll just tell Miri I'm going."

"She knows." Crossing the room, Dillon slid open the glass door and waited for Laine to precede him outside.

Laine found Dillon in a silent mood as they drove from the house. She gave his thoughts their privacy and concentrated on the view. Ridges of green mountains loomed on either side. Dillon drove along a sheer precipice where the earth surrendered abruptly to the sky to fall into an azure sea.

"They used to toss Kukui oil torches over the cliffs to entertain royalty," Dillon said suddenly, after miles of silence. "Legend has it that the menehune lived here. The pixie people," he elaborated at her blank expression. "You see there?" After halting the car, he pointed to a black precipice lined with grooves. "That's their staircase. They built fishponds by moonlight."

"Where are they now?" Laine smiled at him.

Dillon reached across to open her door. "Oh, they're still here. They're hiding."

Laine joined him to walk to the edge of the cliff. Her heart flew to her throat as she stared from the dizzying height down to the frothing power of waves on rock. For an instant, she could feel herself tumbling helplessly through miles of space.

Unaffected by vertigo, Dillon looked out to sea. The breeze teased his hair, tossing it into confusion. "You have the remarkable capacity of knowing when to be quiet and making the silence comfortable," he remarked.

"You seemed preoccupied." The wind tossed curls in her eyes, and Laine brushed them away. "I thought perhaps you were working out a problem."

"Did you?" he returned, and his expression seemed both amused and annoyed. "I want to talk to you about your mother."

The statement was so unexpected that it took Laine a moment to react. "No." She turned away, but he took her arm and held her still.

"You were furious last night. I want to know why."

"I overreacted." She tossed her head as her curls continued to dance around her face. "It was foolish of me, but sometimes my temper gets the better of me." She saw by his expression that her explanation would not placate him. She wanted badly to tell him how she had been hurt, but the memory of their first discussion in her father's house, and his cold judgment of her, prevented her. "Dillon, all my life I've been accepted for who I am." Speaking slowly, she chose her words carefully. "It annoys me to find that changing now. I do not want to be compared with Vanessa because we share certain physical traits."

"Is that what you think Cap was doing?"

"Perhaps, perhaps not." She tilted her chin yet further. "But that's what you were doing."

"Was I?" It was a question which asked for no answer, and Laine gave none. "Why are you so bitter about your mother, Laine?"

She moved her shoulders and turned back toward the sea. "I'm not bitter, Dillon, not any longer. Vanessa's dead, and that part of my life is over. I don't want to talk about her until I understand my feelings better."

"All right." They stood silent for a moment, wrapped in the wind.

"I'm having a lot more trouble with you than I anticipated," Dillon muttered.

"I don't know what you mean."

"No," he agreed, looking at her so intently she felt he read her soul. "I'm sure you don't." He walked away, then stopped. After a hesitation too brief to measure, he turned toward her again and held out his hand. Laine stared at it, unsure what he was offering. Finding it did not matter, she accepted.

During the ensuing drive, Dillon spoke easily. His mood had altered, and Laine moved with it. The world was lush with ripe blossoms. Moss clung, green and vibrant, to cliffs —a carpet on stone. They passed elephant ears whose leaves were large enough to use as a canopy against rain or sun. The frangipani became more varied and more brilliant. When Dillon stopped the car again, Laine did not hesitate to take his hand.

He led her along a path that was sheltered by palms, moving down it as though he knew the way well. Laine heard the rush of water before they entered the clearing. Her breath caught at the sight of the secluded pool circled by thick trees and fed by a shimmering waterfall.

"Oh, Dillon, what a glorious place! There can't be another like it in the world!" Laine ran to the edge of the pool, then dropped down to feel the texture of the water. It was warm silk. "If I could, I would come here to swim in the moonlight." With a laugh, she rose and tossed water to the sky. "With flowers in my hair and nothing else."

"That's the only permissible way to swim in a moonlit pool. Island law."

Laughing again, she turned to a bush and plucked a scarlet hibiscus. "I suppose I'd need long black hair and honey skin to look the part."

Taking the bloom from her, Dillon tucked it behind her ear. After studying the effect, he smiled and ran a finger down her cheek. "Ivory and gold work very nicely. There was a time you'd have been worshiped with all pomp and ceremony, then tossed off a cliff as an offering to jealous gods."

"I don't believe that would suit me." Utterly enchanted, Laine twirled away. "Is this a secret place? It feels like a secret place." Stepping out of her shoes, she sat on the edge of the pool and dangled her feet in the water.

"If you want it to be." Dropping down beside her, Dillon sat Indian fashion. "It's not on the tourist route at any rate."

"It feels magic, the same way that little bay feels magic. Do you feel it, Dillon? Do you realize how lovely this all is, how fresh, or are you immune to it by now?"

"I'm not immune to beauty." He lifted her hand, brushing his lips over her fingertips. Her eyes grew wide as currents of pleasure jolted up her arm. Smiling, Dillon turned her hand over and kissed her palm. "You can't have lived in Paris for fifteen years and not have had your hand kissed. I've seen movies."

The lightness of his tone helped her regain her balance. "Actually, everyone's always kissing my left hand. You threw me off when you kissed my right." She kicked water in the air and watched the drops catch the sun before they were swallowed by the pool. "Sometimes, when the rain drizzles in the fall, and the dampness creeps through the windows, I'll remember this." Her voice had changed, and there was something wistful, something yearning in her tone. "Then when spring comes, and the buds flower, and the air smells of them, I'll remember the fragrance here. And when the sun shines on a Sunday, I'll walk near the Seine and think of a waterfall."

Rain came without warning, a shower drenched in sun. Dillon scrambled up, pulling Laine under a sheltering cluster of palms.

"Oh, it's warm." She leaned out from the green ceiling to catch rain in her palm. "It's as if it's dropping from the sun."

"Islanders call it liquid sunshine." Dillon gave an easy tug on her hand to pull her back as she inched forward. "You're getting soaked. I think you must enjoy getting drenched in your clothes." He ruffled her hair and splattered the air with shimmering drops.

"Yes, I suppose I do." She stared out, absorbed with the deepening colors. Blossoms trembled under their shower. "There's so much on the island that remains unspoiled, as if no one had ever touched it. When we stood on the cliff and looked down at the sea, I was frightened. I've always been a coward. But still, it was beautiful, so terrifyingly beautiful I couldn't look away."

"A coward?" Dillon sat on the soft ground and pulled her down to join him. Her head naturally found the curve of his shoulder. "I would have said you were remarkably intrepid. You didn't panic during the storm yesterday."

"No, I just skirted around the edges of panic."

His laugh was full of pleasure. "You also survived the little show in the plane on the way from Oahu without a scream or a faint."

"That's because I was angry." She pushed at her damp hair and watched the thin curtain of rain. "It was unkind of you."

"Yes, I suppose it was. I'm often unkind."

"I think you're kind more often than not. Though I also think you don't like being labeled a kind man."

"That's a very odd opinion for a short acquaintance." Her answering shrug was eloquent and intensely Gallic. A frown moved across his brow. "This school of yours," he began, "what kind is it?"

"Just a school, the same as any other, with giggling girls and rules which must be broken."

"A boarding school?" he probed, and she moved her shoulders again.

"Yes, a boarding school. Dillon, this is not the place to think of schedules and classes. I shall have to deal with them again soon enough. This is a magic place, and for now I want to pretend I belong here. *Ah, regarde!*" Laine shifted, gesturing in wonder. *"Un arc-en-ciel."*

"I guess that means rainbow." He glanced at the sky, then back at her glowing face.

"There are two! How can there be two?"

They stretched, high and perfect, in curving arches from one mountain ridge to another. The second's shimmering colors were the reverse of the first's. As the sun glistened on raindrops, the colors grew in intensity, streaking across the cerulean sky like a trail from an artist's many-tinted brush.

"Double bows are common here," Dillon explained, relaxing against the base of the palm. "The trade winds blow against the mountains and form a rain boundary. It rains on one side while the sun shines on the other. Then, the sun strikes the raindrops, and . . ."

"No, don't tell me," Laine interrupted with a shake of her head. "It would spoil it if I knew." She smiled with the sudden knowledge that all things precious should be left unexplained. "I don't want to understand," she murmured, accepting both her love and the rainbows without question, without logic. "I just want to enjoy." Tilting back her head, Laine offered her mouth. "Will you kiss me, Dillon?"

His eyes never left hers. He brought his hands to her face, and gently, his fingers stroked the fragile line of her cheek. In silence, he explored the planes and hollows of her face with his fingertips, learning the texture of fine bones and satin skin. His mouth followed the trail of his fingers, and Laine closed her eyes, knowing nothing had ever been sweeter than his lips on her skin. Still moving slowly, still moving gently, Dillon brushed his mouth over hers in a whisperlike kiss which drugged her senses. He seemed content to taste, seemed happy to sample rather than devour. His mouth moved on, lingering on the curve of her neck, nibbling at the lobe of her ear before coming back to join hers. His tongue teased her lips apart as her heartbeat began to roar in her ears. He took her to the edge of reason with a tender, sensitive touch. As her need grew, Laine drew him closer, her body moving against his in innocent temptation.

Dillon swore suddenly before pulling her back. She kept her arms around his neck, her fingers tangled in his hair as he stared down at her. Her eyes were deep and cloudy with growing passion. Unaware of her own seductive powers, Laine sighed his name and placed a soft kiss on both of his cheeks.

"I want you," Dillon stated in a savage murmur before his mouth crushed hers. She yielded to him as a young willow yields to the wind.

His hands moved over her as if desperate to learn every aspect, every secret, and she who had never known a man's intimate touch delighted in the seeking. Her body was limber under his touch, responsive and eager. She was the student, and he the teacher. Her skin grew hot as her veins swelled with pounding blood. As the low, smoldering fire burst into quick flame, her demands rose with his. She trembled and murmured his name, as frightened of the new sensation as she had been at the edge of the cliff.

Dillon lifted his mouth from hers, resting it on her hair before she could search for the joining again. He held her close, cradling her head against his chest. His heart drummed against her ear, and Laine closed her eyes with the pleasure. Drawing her away, he stood. He moved his hands to his pockets as he turned his back on her.

"It's stopped raining." She thought his voice sounded strange and heard him take a long breath before he turned back to her. "We'd better go."

His expression was unfathomable. Though she searched, Laine could find no words to fill the sudden gap and close the distance which had sprung between them. Her eyes met his, asking questions her lips could not. Dillon opened his mouth as if to speak, then closed it again before he reached down to pull her to her feet. Her eyes faltered. Dillon lifted her chin with his fingertips, then traced the lips still soft from his. Briskly, he shook his head. Without a word, he lay his mouth gently on hers before he led her away from the palms.

Chapter Nine

A generous golden ball, the sun dominated the sky as the car moved along the highway. Dillon made easy conversation, as if passion belonged only to a rain-curtained pool. While her brain fidgeted, Laine tried to match his mood.

Men, she decided, must be better able to deal with the demands of the body than women are with those of the heart. He had wanted her; even if he had not said it, she would have known. The urgency, the power of his claim had been unmistakable. Laine felt her color rise as she remembered her unprotesting response. Averting her head as if absorbed in the view, she tried to decide what course lay open to her.

She would leave Kauai in a week's time. Now, she would not only have to abandon the father whom she had longed for all of her life, but the man who held all claim to her heart. Perhaps, she reflected with a small sigh, I'm always destined to love what can never be mine. Miri said I should fight as a woman fights, but I don't know where to begin. Perhaps with honesty. I should find the place and the time to tell Dillon of my feelings. If he knew I wanted nothing from him but his affection, we might make a beginning. I could find a way to stay here at least a while longer. I could take a job. In time, he might learn to really care for me. Laine's mood lightened at the thought. She focused again on her surroundings.

"Dillon, what is growing there? Is it bamboo?" Acres upon acres of towering stalks bordered the road. Clumps of cylindrical gold stretched out on either side.

"Sugarcane," he answered, without glancing at the fields.

"It's like a jungle." Fascinated, Laine leaned out the window, and the wind buffeted her face. "I had no idea it grew so tall."

"Gets to be a bit over twenty feet, but it doesn't grow as fast as a jungle in this part of the world. It takes a year and a half to two years to reach full growth."

"There's so much." Laine turned to face him, absently brushing curls from her cheeks. "It's a plantation, I suppose, though it's hard to conceive of one person owning so much. It must take tremendous manpower to harvest."

"A bit." Dillon swerved off the highway and onto a hard-packed road. "The undergrowth is burned off, then machines cut the plants. Hand cutting is time consuming so machinery lowers production costs even when labor costs are low. Besides, it's one miserable job."

"Have you ever done it?" She watched a quick grin light his face.

"A time or two, which is why I prefer flying a plane."

Laine gazed around at the infinity of fields, wondering when the harvest began, trying to picture the machines slicing through the towering stalks. Her musings halted as the brilliant white of a house shone in the distance. Tall, with graceful colonial lines and pillars, it stood on lush lawns. Vines dripped from scrolled balconies; the high and narrow windows were shuttered in soft gray. The house looked comfortably old and lived in. Had it not been for South Sea foliage, Laine might have been seeing a plantation house in old Louisiana.

"What a beautiful home. One could see for miles from the balcony." Laine glanced at Dillon in surprise as he halted the car and again leaned over to open her door. "This is a private home, is it not? Are we allowed to walk around?"

"Sure." Opening his own door, Dillon slid out. "It's mine." He leaned against the car and looked down at her. "Are you going to sit there with your mouth open or are you going to come inside?" Quickly, Laine slid out and stood beside him. "I gather you expected a grass hut and hammock?"

"Why, no, I don't know precisely what I expected, but . . ." With a helpless gesture of her hands, she gazed about. A tremor of alarm trickled through her. "The cane fields," she began, praying she was mistaken. "Are they yours?"

"They go with the house."

Finding her throat closed, Laine said nothing as Dillon led her up stone steps and through a wide mahogany door. Inside, the staircase dominated the hall. Wide and arching in a deep half circle, its wood gleamed. Laine had a quick, confused impression of watercolors and wood carvings as Dillon strode straight down the hall and led her into a parlor.

The walls were like rich cream; the furnishings were dark and old. The carpet was a delicately faded needlepoint over a glistening wood floor. Nutmeg sheers were drawn back from the windows to allow the view of a manicured lawn.

"Sit down." Dillon gestured to a chair. "I'll see about something cold to drink." Laine nodded, grateful for the time alone to organize her scattered thoughts. She listened until Dillon's footsteps echoed into silence.

Her survey of the room was slow. She

seated herself in a high-backed chair and let her eyes roam. The room had an undeniable air of muted wealth. Laine had not associated wealth with Dillon O'Brian. Now she found it an insurmountable obstacle. Her protestations of love would never be accepted as pure. He would think his money had been her enticement. She closed her eyes on a small moan of desperation. Rising, she moved to a window and tried to deal with dashed hopes.

What was it he called me once? *An operator*. With a short laugh, she rested her brow against the cool glass. I'm afraid I make a very poor one. I wish I'd never come here, never seen what he has. At least then I could have hung onto hope a bit longer. Hearing Dillon's approach, Laine struggled for composure. As he entered, she gave him a careful smile.

"Dillon, your home is very lovely." After accepting the tall glass he offered, Laine moved back to her chair.

"It serves." He sat opposite her. His brow lifted fractionally at the formality of her tone.

"Did you build it yourself?"

"No, my grandfather." With his customary ease, Dillon leaned back and watched her. "He was a sailor and decided Kauai was the next best thing to the sea."

"So. I thought it looked as if it had known generations." Laine sipped at her drink without tasting it. "But you found planes more enticing than the sea or the fields."

"The fields serve their purpose." Dillon frowned momentarily at her polite, impersonal interest. "They yield a marketable product, assist in local employment and make use of the land. It's a profitable crop and its management takes only a portion of my time." As Dillon set down his glass, Laine thought he appeared to come to some decision. "My father died a couple of months before I met Cap. We were both floundering, but I was angry, and he was . . ." Dillon hesitated, then shrugged. "He was as he always is. We suited each other. He had a cabin plane and used to pick up island hoppers. I couldn't learn about flying fast enough, and Cap needed to teach. I needed balance, and he needed to give it. A couple of years later, we began planning the airport."

Laine dropped her eyes to her glass. "And it was the money from your fields which built the airport?"

"As I said, the cane has its uses."

"And the bay where we swam?" On a sudden flash of intuition, she lifted her eyes to his. "That's yours too, isn't it?"

"That's right." She could see no change of expression in his eyes.

"And my father's house?" Laine swallowed the dryness building in her throat. "Is that also on your property?"

She saw annoyance cross his face before he smoothed it away. His answer was mild. "Cap had a fondness for that strip of land, so he bought it."

"From you?"

"Yes, from me. Is that a problem?"

"No," she replied. "It's simply that I begin to see things more clearly. Much more clearly." Laine set down her drink and folded her empty hands. "It appears that you are more my father's son than I shall ever be his daughter."

"Laine . . ." Dillon let out a short breath, then rose and paced the room with a sudden restlessness. "Cap and I understand each other. We've known each other for nearly fifteen years. He's been part of my life for almost half of it."

"I'm not asking you for justifications, Dillon. I'm sorry if it seemed as if I were." Laine stood, trying to keep her voice steady. "When I return to France next week, it will be good to know that my father has you to rely on."

"Next week?" Dillon stopped pacing. "You're planning to leave next week?"

"Yes." Laine tried not to think of how quickly seven days could pass. "We agreed I would stay for two weeks. It's time I got back to my own life."

"You're hurt because Cap hasn't responded to you the way you'd hoped."

Surprised both by his words and the gentleness of his tone, Laine felt the thin thread of her control straining. She struggled to keep her eyes calm and level with his. "I have changed my mind . . . on a great many matters. Please don't, Dillon." She shook her head as he started to speak. "I would rather not talk of this; it's only more difficult."

"Laine." He placed his hands on her shoulders to prevent her from turning away. "There are a lot of things that you and I have to talk about, whether they're difficult or not. You can't keep shutting away little parts of yourself. I want . . ." The ringing of the doorbell interrupted his words. With a quick, impatient oath, he dropped his hands and strode away to answer.

A light, musical voice drifted into the room. When Orchid King entered the parlor on Dillon's arm, Laine met her with a polite smile.

It struck Laine that Orchid and Dillon were a perfectly matched couple. Orchid's tawny, exotic beauty suited his ruggedness, and her fully rounded curves were all the more stunning against his leanness. Her hair fell in an ebony waterfall, cascading down a smooth bare back to the waist of close-fitting, pumpkin-colored shorts. Seeing her, Laine felt dowdy and provincial.

"Hello, Miss Simmons." Orchid tightened her hand on Dillon's arm. "How nice to see you again so soon."

"Hello, Miss King." Annoyed by her own insecurities, Laine met Orchid's amusement with eyes of a cool spring morning. "You did say the island was small."

"Yes, I did." She smiled, and Laine was reminded of a tawny cat. "I hope you've been able to see something of it."

"I took Laine around a bit this morning." Watching Laine, Dillon missed the flash of fire in Orchid's amber eyes.

"I'm sure she couldn't find a better guide." Orchid's expression melted into soft appeal. "I'm so glad you were home, Dillon. I wanted to make certain you'd be at the luau tomorrow night." Turning more directly to face him, she subtly but effectively excluded Laine from the conversation. "It wouldn't be any fun without you."

"I'll be there." Laine watched a smile lift one corner of his mouth. "Are you going to dance?"

"Of course." The soft purr of her voice added to Laine's image of a lithesome feline. "Tommy expects it."

Dillon's smile flashed into a grin. He lifted his eyes over Orchid's head to meet Laine's. "Tommy is Miri's nephew. He's having his annual luau tomorrow. You should find both the food and the entertainment interesting."

"Oh yes," Orchid agreed. "No tourist should leave the islands without attending a luau. Do you plan to see the other islands during your vacation?"

"I'm afraid that will have to wait for another time. I'm sorry to say I haven't lived up to my obligations as a tourist. The purpose of my visit has been to see my father and his home."

Somewhat impatiently, Dillon disengaged his arm from Orchid's grasp. "I have to see my foreman. Why don't you keep Laine company for a few minutes?"

"Certainly." Orchid tossed a lock of rain-straight hair behind her back. "How are the repairs coming?"

"Fine. I should be able to move back in a couple of days without being in the way." With an inclination of his head for Laine, he turned and strode from the room.

"Miss Simmons, do make yourself at home." Assuming the role of hostess with a graceful wave of her hand, Orchid glided further into the room. "Would you care for anything? A cold drink perhaps?"

Infuriated at being placed in the position of being Orchid's guest, Laine forced down her temper. "Thank you, no. Dillon has already seen to it."

"It seems you spend a great deal of time in Dillon's company," Orchid commented as she dropped into a chair. She crossed long, slender legs, looking like an advertisement for Hawaii's lush attractions. "Especially for one who comes to visit her father."

"Dillon has been very generous with his time." Laine copied Orchid's action and hoped she was equipped for a feminine battle of words.

"Oh yes, Dillon's a generous man." Her smile was indulgent and possessive. "It's quite easy to misinterpret his generosity unless one knows him as well as I do. He can be so charming."

"Charming?" Laine repeated, and looked faintly skeptical. "How odd. Charming is not the adjective which comes to my mind. But then," she paused and smiled, "you know him better than I do."

Orchid placed the tips of her fingers together, then regarded Laine over the tips. "Miss Simmons, maybe we can dispense with the polite small talk while we have this time alone."

Wondering if she was sinking over her head, Laine nodded. "Your option, Miss King."

"I intend to marry Dillon."

"A formidable intention," Laine managed as her heart constricted. "I assume Dillon is aware of your goal."

"Dillon knows I want him." Irritation flickered over the exotic face at Laine's easy answer. "I don't appreciate all the time you've been spending with him."

"That's a pity, Miss King." Laine picked up her long-abandoned glass and sipped. "But don't you think you're discussing this with the wrong person? I'm sure speaking to Dillon would be more productive."

"I don't believe that's necessary." Orchid gave Laine a companionable smile, showing just a hint of white teeth. "I'm sure we can settle this between us. Don't you think telling Dillon you wanted to learn to fly a plane was a little trite?"

Laine felt a rush of fury that Dillon had discussed her with Orchid. "Trite?"

Orchid made an impatient gesture. "Dillon's diverted by you at the moment, perhaps because you're such a contrast to the type of woman he's always preferred. But milk-and-honey looks won't keep Dillon interested for long." The musical voice hardened. "Cool sophistication doesn't keep a man warm, and Dillon is very much a man."

"Yes, he's made that very clear," Laine could not resist interjecting.

"I'm warning you . . . once," Orchid hissed. "Keep your distance. I can make things very uncomfortable for you."

"I'm sure you can," Laine acknowledged. She shrugged. "I've been uncomfortable before."

"Dillon can be very vindictive when he thinks he's been deceived. You're going to end up losing more than you bargained for."

"*Nom de Dieu!*" Laine rose. "Is this how the game is played?" She made a contemptuous gesture with the back of her hand. "I want none of it. Snarling and hissing like two cats over a mouse. This isn't worthy of Dillon."

"We haven't started to play yet." Orchid sat back, pleased by Laine's agitation. "If you don't like the rules, you'd better leave. I don't intend to put up with you any longer."

"Put up with me?" Laine stopped, her voice trembling with rage. "No one, Miss King, no one *puts up* with me. You hardly need concern yourself with a woman who will be gone in a week's time. Your lack of confidence is as pitiful as your threats." Orchid rose at that, her fists clenched by her sides.

"What do you want from me?" Laine demanded. "Do you want my assurance that I won't interfere with your plans? Very well, I give it freely and with pleasure. Dillon is yours."

"That's generous of you." Spinning, Laine saw Dillon leaning against the doorway. His arms were crossed, his eyes dangerously dark.

"Oh, Dillon, how quick you were." Orchid's voice was faint.

"Apparently not quick enough." His eyes were locked on Laine's. "What's the problem?"

"Just a little feminine talk, Dillon." Recovered, Orchid glided to his side. "Laine and I were just getting to know each other."

"Laine, what's going on?"

"Nothing important. If it's convenient, I should like to go back now." Without waiting for a reply, Laine picked up her bag and moved to the doorway.

Dillon halted her by a hand on her arm. "I asked you a question."

"And I have given you the only answer I intend to give." She wrenched free and faced him. "I will not be questioned any longer. You have no right to question me; I am nothing to you. You have no right to criticize me as you have done from the first moment. You have no right to judge." The anger in her tone was now laced with despair. "You have no right to make love to me just because it amuses you."

She ran in a flurry of flying skirts, and he watched the door slam behind her.

Chapter Ten

Laine spent the rest of the day in her room. She attempted not to dwell on the scene in Dillon's home, or on the silent drive which followed it. She was not sure which had been more draining. It occurred to her that she and Dillon never seemed to enjoy a cordial relationship for more than a few hours at a time. It was definitely time to leave. She began to plan for her return to France. Upon a review of her finances, she discovered that she had barely enough for a return ticket.

It would, she realized with a sigh, leave her virtually penniless. Her own savings had been sorely dented in dealing with her mother's debts, and plane fare had eaten at what remained. She could not, she determined, return to France without a franc in her pocket. If there was a complication of any kind, she would be helpless to deal with it. *Why didn't I stop to think before I came here*? she demanded of herself. *Now I've placed myself in an impossible situation.*

Sitting on the bed, Laine rubbed an aching temple and tried to think. She didn't want to ask her father for money. Pride prevented her from wiring to any friends to ask for a loan. She stared down at the small pile of bills in frustration. They won't proliferate of their own accord, she reflected, so I must plan how to increase their number.

She moved to her dresser and opened a small box. For some minutes, she studied the gold locket it contained. It had been a gift from her father to her mother, and Vanessa had given it to her on her sixteenth birthday. She remembered the pleasure she had felt upon receiving something, however indirectly, from her father. She had worn it habitually until she had dressed for her flight to Hawaii. Feeling it might cause her father pain, Laine had placed it in its box, hoping that unhappy memories would be buried. It was the only thing of value she owned, and now she had to sell it.

Her door swung open. Laine held the box behind her back. Miri glided in, a swirling mountain of color. She regarded Laine's flushed face with raised brows.

"Did you mess something up?"

"No."

"Then don't look guilty. Here." She laid a sheath of brilliant blue and sparkling white on the bedspread. "It's for you. You wear this to the luau tomorrow."

"Oh." Laine stared at the exquisite length of silk, already feeling its magic against her skin. "It's beautiful. I couldn't." She raised her eyes to Miri's with a mixture of desire and regret. "I couldn't take it."

"You don't like my present?" Miri demanded imperiously. "You are very rude."

"Oh no." Struck with alarm at the unintentional offense, Laine fumbled with an explanation. "It's beautiful . . . really. It's only that . . ."

"You should learn to say thank you and not argue. This will suit your skinny bones." Miri gave a nod of satisfaction encompassing both the woman and the silk. "Tomorrow, I will show you how to wrap it."

Unable to prevent herself, Laine moved over to feel the cool material under her fingers. The combination of longing and Miri's dark, arched brows proved too formidable for pride. She surrendered with a sigh. "Thank you, Miri. It's very good of you."

"That's much better," Miri approved and patted Laine's halo of curls. "You are a pretty child. You should smile more. When you smile, the sadness goes away."

Feeling the small box weighing like a stone in her hand, Laine held it up and opened it.

"Miri, I wonder if you might tell me where I could sell this."

One large brown finger traced the gold before Miri's jet eyes lifted. Laine saw the now familiar pucker between her brows. "Why do you want to sell a pretty thing like this? You don't like it?"

"No, no, I like it very much." Helpless under the direct stare, Laine moved her shoulders. "I need the money."

"Money? Why do you need money?"

"For my passage and expenses . . . to return to France."

"You don't like Kauai?" Her indignant tone caused Laine to smile and shake her head.

"Kauai is wonderful; I'd like nothing better than to stay here forever. But I must get back to my job."

"What do you do in that place?" Miri dismissed France with a regal gesture and settled her large frame into a chair. She folded her hands across the mound of her belly.

"I teach." Laine sat on the bed and closed the lid on the face of the locket.

"Don't they pay you to teach?" Miri pursed her lips in disapproval. "What did you do with your money?"

Laine flushed, feeling like a child who had been discovered spending her allowance on candy. "There . . . there were debts, and I . . ."

"You have debts?"

"Well, no, I . . . not precisely." Laine's

shoulders drooped with frustration. Seeing Miri was prepared to remain a permanent fixture of her room until she received an explanation, Laine surrendered. Slowly, she began to explain the financial mountain which she had faced at her mother's death, the necessity to liquidate assets, the continuing drain on her own resources. In the telling, Laine felt the final layers of her resentment fading. Miri did not interrupt the recital, and Laine found that confession had purged her of bitterness.

"Then, when I found my father's address among her personal papers, I took what I had left and came here. I'm afraid I didn't plan things well, and in order to go back . . ." She shrugged again and trailed off. Miri nodded.

"Why have you not told Cap Simmons? He would not have his daughter selling baubles. He's a good man, he would not have you in a strange country counting your pennies."

"He doesn't owe me anything."

"He is your father," Miri stated, lifting her chin and peering at Laine down her nose.

"But he's not responsible for a situation brought on by Vanessa's carelessness and my own impulsiveness. He would think . . . No." She shook her head. "I don't want him to know. It's very important to me that he *not* know. You must promise not to speak of this to him."

"You are a very stubborn girl." Miri crossed her arms and glared at Laine. Laine kept her eyes level. "Very well." Miri's bosom lifted and fell with her sigh. "You must do what you must do. Tomorrow, you will meet my nephew, Tommy. Ask him to come look at your bauble. He is a jeweler and will give you a fair price."

"Thank you, Miri." Laine smiled, feeling a portion of her burden ease.

Miri rose, her muumuu trembling at the movement. "You had a nice day with Dillon?"

"We went by his home," Laine returned evasively. "It's very impressive."

"Very nice place," Miri agreed and brushed an infinitesimal speck of dust from the chair's back. "My cousin cooks there, but not so well as Miri."

"Miss King dropped by." Laine strove for a casual tone, but Miri's brows rose.

"Hmph." Miri stroked the tentlike lines of her flowered silk.

"We had a rather unpleasant discussion when Dillon left us alone. When he came back . . ." Laine paused and drew her brows together. "I shouted at him."

Miri laughed, holding her middle as if it would split from the effort. For several moments, her mirth rolled comfortably around the room. "So you can shout, Skinny Bones? I would like to have seen that."

"I don't think Dillon found it that amusing." In spite of herself, Laine smiled.

"Oh, that one." She wiped her eyes and shook her head. "He is too used to having his own way with women. He is too good-looking and has too much money." She placed a comforting hand over the barrel of her belly. "He's a fair boss, and he works in the fields when he's needed. He has big degrees and many brains." She tapped her finger on her temple, but looked unimpressed. "He was a very bad boy, with many pranks." Laine saw her lips tremble as she tried not to show amusement at the memories. "He is still a bad boy," she said firmly, regaining her dignity. "He is very smart and *very* important." She made a circling movement with both hands to indicate Dillon's importance, but her voice was full of maternal criticism. "But no matter what he thinks, he does not know women. He only knows planes." She patted Laine's head and pointed to the length of silk. "Tomorrow, you wear that and put a flower in your hair. The moon will be full."

It was a night of silver and velvet. From her window, Laine could see the dancing diamonds of moonlight on the sea. Allowing the breeze to caress her bare shoulders, Laine reflected that the night was perfect for a luau under the stars.

She had not seen Dillon since the previous day. He had returned to the house long after she had retired, and had left again before she had awakened. She was determined, however, not to permit their last meeting to spoil the beauty of the evening. If she had only a few days left in his company, she would make every effort to see that they were pleasant.

Turning from the window, Laine gave one final look at the woman in the mirror. Her bare shoulders rose like marble from the brilliant blue of the sarong. She stared at the woman in the glass, recognizing some change, but unable to discern its cause. She was not aware that over the past few days she had moved from girlhood to womanhood. After a final touch of the brush to her hair, Laine left the room. Dillon's voice rose up the staircase, and she moved to meet it. All at once, it seemed years since she had last heard him speak.

"We'll be harvesting next month, but if I know the schedule of meetings far enough in advance, I can . . ."

His voice trailed away as Laine moved into the doorway. Pausing in the act of pouring a drink, he made a slow survey. Laine felt her pulse triple its rate as his eyes lingered along their route before meeting hers.

Glancing up from filling his pipe, Cap noted Dillon's absorption. He followed his gaze. "Well, Laine." He rose, surprising her by crossing the room and taking both her hands in his. "What a beautiful sight."

"Do you like it?" Smiling first at him, she glanced down at the sarong. "I'm not quite used to the way it feels."

"I like it very much, but I was talking about you. My daughter is a very beautiful woman, isn't she, Dillon?" His eyes were soft and smiled into Laine's.

"Yes," Dillon's voice came from behind him. "Very beautiful."

"I'm glad she's here." He pressed her fingers between the warmth of his hands. "I've missed her." He bent and kissed her cheek, then turned to Dillon. "You two run along. I'll see if Miri's ready, which she won't be. We'll be along later."

Laine watched him stride away. She lifted one hand to her cheek, unable to believe she could be so deeply affected by one small gesture.

"Are you ready?" She nodded, unable to speak, then felt Dillon's hands descend to her shoulders. "It isn't easy to bridge a fifteen-year gap, but you've made a start."

Surprised by the support in his voice, Laine blinked back tears and turned to face him. "Thank you. It means a great deal to me for you to say that. Dillon, yesterday I . . ."

"Let's not worry about yesterday right now." His smile was both an apology and an acceptance of hers. It was easy to smile back. He studied her a moment before lifting her hand to his lips. "You are incredibly beautiful, like a blossom hanging on a branch just out of reach." Laine wanted to blurt out that she was not out of reach, but a thick blanket of shyness covered her tongue. She could do no more than stare at him.

"Come on." Keeping her hand in his, Dillon

moved to the door. "You should try everything once." His tone was light again as they slid into his car. "You know, you're a very small lady."

"Only because you look from an intimidating height," she returned, feeling pleased with the ease of their relationship. "What does one do at a luau, Dillon? I'm very much afraid I'll insult a local tradition if I refuse to eat raw fish. But"—resting her head against the seat, she smiled at the stars—"I shall refuse to do so."

"We don't hurl mainlanders into the sea any more for minor offenses. You haven't much hip," he commented, dropping his eyes for a moment. "But you could have a stab at a hula."

"I'm sure my hips are adequate and will no doubt be more so if Miri has her way." Laine sent him a teasing glance. "Do you dance, Dillon?"

He grinned and met her look. "I prefer to watch. Dancing the hula properly takes years of practice. These dancers are very good."

"I see." She shifted in her seat to smile at him. "Will there be many people at the luau?"

"Mmm." Dillon tapped his finger absently against the wheel. "About a hundred, give or take a few."

"A hundred," Laine echoed. She fought off unhappy memories of her mother's overcrowded, overelegant parties. So many people, so many demands, so many measuring eyes.

"Tommy has a lot of relatives."

"How nice for him," she murmured and considered the advantages of small families.

Chapter Eleven

The hollow, primitive sound of drums vibrated through air pungent with roasting meat. Torches were set on high stakes, their orange flames shooting flickering light against a black sky. To Laine it was like stepping back in time. The lawn was crowded with guests—some in traditional attire and others, like Dillon, in the casual comfort of jeans. Laughter rose from a myriad of tones and mixed languages. Laine gazed around, enthralled by the scene and the scents.

Set on a huge, woven mat were an infinite variety of mysterious dishes in wooden bowls and trays. Ebony-haired girls in native dress knelt to spoon food onto the plates and serving dishes. Diverse aromas lifted on the night air and lingered to entice. Men, swathed at the waist and bare-chested, beat out pulsating rhythms on high, conical drums.

Introduced to an impossible blur of faces, Laine merely floated with the mood of the crowd. There seemed to be a universal friendliness, an uncomplicated joy in simply being.

Soon sandwiched between her father and Dillon, Laine sat on the grass and watched her plate being heaped with unknown wonders. A roar of approval rose over the music as the pig was unearthed from the *imu* and carved. Dutifully, she dipped her fingers in *poi* and sampled. She shrugged her shoulders as Dillon laughed at her wrinkled nose.

"Perhaps it's an acquired taste," she suggested as she wiped her fingers on a napkin.

"Here." Dillon lifted a fork and urged its contents into Laine's reluctant mouth.

With some surprise, she found the taste delightful. "That's very good. What is it?"

"Laulau."

"That is not illuminating."

"If it's good, what else do you have to know?" His logic caused her to arch her brows. "It's pork and butterfish steamed in ti leaves," he explained, shaking his head. "Try this." Dillon offered the fork again, and Laine accepted without hesitation.

"Oh, what is it? I've never tasted anything like it."

"Squid," he answered, then roared with laughter at her gasp of alarm.

"I believe," Laine stated with dignity, "I shall limit myself to pork and pineapple."

"You'll never grow hips that way."

"I shall learn to live without them. What is this drink . . . ? No," she decided, smiling as she heard her father's chuckle. "I believe I'm better off not knowing."

Avoiding the squid, Laine found herself enjoying the informal meal. Occasionally, someone stopped and crouched beside them, exchanging quick greetings or a long story. Laine was treated with a natural friendliness which soon put her at her ease. Her father seemed comfortable with her, and though he and Dillon enjoyed an *entente* which eluded her, she no longer felt like an intruder. Music and laughter and the heady perfume of night swam around her. Laine thought she had never felt so intensely aware of her surroundings.

Suddenly, the drummers beat a rapid tempo, reaching a peak, then halting. Their echo fell into silence as Orchid stepped into view. She stood in a circle of torchlight, her skin glowing under its touch. Her eyes were gold and arrogant. Tantalizing and perfect, her body was adorned only in a brief top and a slight swatch of scarlet silk draped low over her hips. She stood completely still, allowing the silence to build before she began slowly circling her hips. A single drum began to follow the rhythm she set.

Her hair, crowned with a circlet of buds, fell

down her bare back. Her hands and lithesome curves moved with a hypnotic power as the bare draping of silk flowed against her thighs. Sensuous and tempting, her gestures moved with the beat, and Laine saw that her golden eyes were locked on Dillon's. The faint smile she gave him was knowledgeable. Almost imperceptibly, her dance grew in speed. As the drum became more insistent, her movements became more abandoned. Her face remained calm and smiling above her undulating body. Then, abruptly, sound and movement halted into stunning silence.

Applause broke out. Orchid threw Laine a look of triumph before she lifted the flower crown from her head and tossed it into Dillon's lap. With a soft, sultry laugh, she retreated to the shadows.

"Looks like you've got yourself an invitation," Cap commented, then pursed his lips in thought. "Amazing. I wonder how many RPMs we could clock her at."

Shrugging, Dillon lifted his glass.

"You like to move like that, Skinny Bones?" Laine turned to where Miri sat in the background. She looked more regal than ever in a high-backed rattan chair. "You eat so you don't rattle, and Miri will teach you."

Flushed with a mixture of embarrassment and the longing to move with such free abandon, Laine avoided Dillon's eyes. "I don't rattle now, but I think Miss King's ability is natural."

"You might pick it up, Duchess." Dillon grinned at Laine's lowered lashes. "I'd like to sit in on the lessons, Miri. As you well know, I've got a very discerning eye." He dropped his gaze to her bare legs, moving it up the length of blue and white silk, before meeting her eyes.

Miri muttered something in Hawaiian, and Dillon chuckled and tossed back a retort in the same tongue. "Come with me," Miri commanded. Rising, she pulled Laine to her feet.

"What did you say to him?" Laine moved in the wake of Miri's flowing gown.

"I said he is a big hungry cat cornering a small mouse."

"I am not a mouse," Laine returned indignantly.

Miri laughed without breaking stride. "Dillon says no, too. He says you are a bird whose beak is sometimes sharp under soft feathers."

"Oh." Unsure whether to be pleased or annoyed with the description, Laine lapsed into silence.

"I have told Tommy you have a bauble to sell," Miri announced. "You will talk to him now."

"Yes, of course," Laine murmured, having forgotten the locket in the enchantment of the night.

Miri paused in front of the luau's host. He was a spare, dark-haired man with an easy smile and friendly eyes. Laine judged him to be in the later part of his thirties, and she had seen him handle his guests with a practiced charm. "You will talk to Cap Simmons's daughter," Miri commanded as she placed a protective hand on Laine's shoulder. "You do right by her, or I will box your ears."

"Yes, Miri," he agreed, but his subservient nod was not reflected in his laughing eyes. He watched the graceful mountain move off before he tossed an arm around Laine's shoulders. He moved her gently toward the privacy of trees. "Miri is the matriarch of our family," he said with a laugh. "She rules with an iron hand."

"Yes, I've noticed. It's impossible to say no to her, isn't it?" The celebrating sounds of the luau drifted into a murmur as they walked.

"I've never tried. I'm a coward."

"I appreciate your time, Mr. Kinimoko," Laine began.

"Tommy, please, then I can call you Laine." She smiled, and as they walked on, she heard the whisper of the sea. "Miri said you had a bauble to sell. I'm afraid she wasn't any more specific."

"A gold locket," Laine explained, finding his friendly manner had put her at ease. "It's heart-shaped and has a braided chain. I have no idea of its value." She paused, wishing there were another way. "I need the money."

Tommy glanced at the delicate profile, then patted her shoulder. "I take it you don't want

Cap to know? O.K.," he continued as she shook her head. "I have some free time in the morning. Why don't I come by and have a look around ten? You'll find it more comfortable than coming into the shop."

Laine heard leaves rustle and saw Tommy glance idly toward the sound. "It's very good of you." He turned back to her and she smiled, relieved that the first hurdle was over. "I hope I'm not putting you to any trouble."

"I enjoy troubling for beautiful *wahines.*" He kept his arm over her shoulders as he led her back toward the sound of drums and guitars. "You heard Miri. You don't want me to get my ears boxed, do you?"

"I would never forgive myself if I were responsible for that. I'll tell Miri you've done right by Cap Simmons's daughter, and your ears will be left in peace." Laughing, Laine tilted her face to his as they broke through the curtain of trees.

"Your sister's looking for you, Tommy." At Dillon's voice, Laine gave a guilty start.

"Thanks, Dillon. I'll just turn Laine over to you. Take good care of her," he advised gravely. "She's under Miri's protection."

"I'll keep that in mind." Dillon watched in silence as Tommy merged back into the crowd, then he turned back to study Laine. "There's an old Hawaiian custom," he began slowly, and she heard annoyance color his tone, "which I have just invented. When a woman comes to a luau with a man, she doesn't walk in monkeypod trees with anyone else."

"Will I be tossed to the sharks if I break the rules?" Her teasing smile faded as Dillon took a step closer.

"Don't, Laine." He circled her neck with his hand. "I haven't much practice in restraint."

She swayed toward him, giving in to the sudden surging need. "Dillon," she murmured, offering her mouth in simple invitation. She felt the strength of his fingers as they tightened on her neck. She rested her hands against his chest and felt his heartbeat under her palms. The knowledge of his power over her, and her own longing, caused her to tremble. Dillon made a soft sound, a lingering expulsion of breath. Laine watched him struggle with some emotion, watched something flicker in his eyes and fade before his fingers relaxed again.

"A *wahine* who stands in the shadows under a full moon must be kissed."

"Is this another old Hawaiian tradition?" Laine felt his arms slip around her waist and melted against him.

"Yes, about ten seconds old."

With unexpected gentleness, his mouth met hers. At the first touch, her body went fluid, mists of pleasure shrouding her. As from a distant shore, Laine heard the call of the drums, their rhythm building to a crescendo as did her heartbeat. Feeling the tenseness of Dillon's shoulders under her hands, she stroked, then circled his neck to bring his face closer to hers. Too soon, he lifted his mouth, and his arms relinquished his hold of her.

"More," Laine murmured, unsatisfied, and pulled his face back to hers.

She was swept against him. The power of his kiss drove all but the need from her mind. She could taste the hunger on his lips, feel the heat growing on his flesh. The air seemed to tremble around them. In that moment, her body belonged more to him than to her. If there was a world apart from seeking lips and caressing hands it held no meaning for her. Again, Dillon drew her away, but his voice was low and uneven.

"We'll go back before another tradition occurs to me."

In the morning, Laine lingered under the sun's streaming light, unwilling to leave her bed and the warm pleasure which still clung from the evening before. The taste of Dillon's mouth still lingered on hers, and his scent remained fresh and vital on her senses. She relived the memory of being in his arms. Finally, with a sigh, she abandoned the luxury of her bed and rose to face the day. Just as she was securing the belt of her robe, Miri glided into the room.

"So, you have decided to get up. The morning is half gone while you lay in your bed." Miri's voice was stern, but her eyes twinkled with indulgence.

"It made the night last longer," Laine replied, smiling at the affectionate scold.

"You liked the roast pig and poi?" Miri asked with a wise nod and a whisper of a smile.

"It was wonderful."

With her lilting laugh floating through the room, Miri turned to leave. "I am going to the market. My nephew is here to see your bauble. Do you want him to wait?"

"Oh." Forcing herself back down to earth, Laine ran her fingers through her hair. "I didn't realize it was that late. I don't want to inconvenience him. I . . . is anyone else at home?"

"No, they are gone."

Glancing down at her robe, Laine decided it was adequate coverage. "Perhaps he could come up and look at it. I don't want to keep him waiting."

"He will give you a fair price," Miri stated as she drifted through the doorway. "Or, you will tell me."

Laine took the small box from her drawer and opened the lid. The locket glinted under a ray of sunshine. There were no pictures to remove but, nonetheless, she opened it and stared at its emptiness.

"Laine."

Turning, she managed to smile at Tommy as he stood in the doorway. "Hello. It was good of you to come. Forgive me, I slept rather late this morning."

"A compliment to the host of the luau." He made a small, rather dapper bow as she approached him.

"It was my first, and I have no doubt it will remain my favorite." Laine handed him the box, then gripped her hands together as he made his examination.

"It's a nice piece," he said at length. Lifting his eyes, Tommy studied her. "Laine, you don't want to sell this—it's written all over your face."

"No." She saw from his manner she need not hedge. "It's necessary that I do."

Detecting the firmness in her voice, Tommy shrugged and placed the locket back in its box. "I can give you a hundred for it, though I think it's worth a great deal more to you."

Laine nodded and closed the lid as he handed the box back to her. "That will be fine. Perhaps you'd take it now. I would rather you kept it."

"If that's what you want." Tommy drew out his wallet and counted out bills. "I brought some cash. I thought you'd find it easier than a check."

"Thank you." After accepting the money, Laine stared down at it until he rested a hand on her shoulder.

"Laine, I've known Cap a long time. Would you take this as a loan?"

"No." She shook her head, then smiled to ease the sharpness of the word. "No. It's very kind of you, but I must do it this way."

"O.K." He took the offered box and pocketed it. "I will, however, hold this for a while in case you have second thoughts."

"Thank you. Thank you for not asking questions."

"I'll see myself out." He took her hand and gave it a small squeeze. "Just tell Miri to get in touch with me if you change your mind."

"Yes, I will."

After he had gone, Laine sat heavily on the bed and stared at the money she held clutched in her hand. There was nothing else I could do, she told herself. It was only a piece of metal. Now, it's done, I can't dwell on it.

"Well, Duchess, it seems you've had a profitable morning."

Laine's head snapped up. Dillon's eyes were frosted like an ice-crusted lake, and she stared at him, unable to clear her thoughts. His gaze raked her scantily clad body, and she reached a hand to the throat of her robe in an automatic gesture. Moving toward her, he pulled the bills from her hand and dropped the money on the nightstand.

"You've got class, Duchess." Dillon pinned her with his eyes. "I'd say that's pretty good for a morning's work."

"What are you talking about?" Her thoughts were scattered as she searched for a way to avoid telling him about the locket.

"Oh, I think that's clear enough. I guess I owe Orchid an apology." He thrust his hands in his pockets and rocked back on his heels.

The easy gesture belied the burning temper in his eyes. "When she told me about this little arrangement, I came down on her pretty hard. You're a fast worker, Laine. You couldn't have been with Tommy for more than ten minutes last night; you must have made quite a sales pitch."

"I don't know why you're so angry," she began, confused as to why the sale of her locket would bring on such fury. "I suppose Miss King listened to our conversation last night." Suddenly, Laine remembered the quick rustle of leaves. "But why she should feel it necessary to report to you on my business . . ."

"How'd you manage to get rid of Miri while you conducted your little business transaction?" Dillon demanded. "She has a rather strict moral code, you know. If she finds out how you're earning your pin money, she's liable to toss you out on your ear."

"What do you . . ." Realization dawned slowly. *Not my locket,* Laine thought dumbly, *but myself.* All trace of color fled from her face. "You don't really believe that I . . ." Her voice broke as she read the condemnation in his eyes. "This is despicable of you, Dillon. Nothing you've accused me of, nothing you've said to me since we first met compares with this." The words trembled with emotion as she felt a vicelike pressure around her heart. "I won't be insulted this way by you."

"Oh, won't you." Taking her arm, Dillon

dragged Laine to her feet. "Have you a more plausible explanation up your sleeve for Tommy's visit and the wad you were fondling? Go ahead, run it by me. I'm listening."

"Oh, yes, I can see you are. Forgive me for refusing, but both Tommy's visit and my money are my business. I owe you no explanations, Dillon. Your conclusions aren't worthy of my words. The fact that you gave enough credence to whatever lie Orchid told you to come check on me, means we have nothing more to say to each other."

"I didn't come here to check on you." He was towering menacingly over her, but Laine met his eyes without flinching. "I came by because I thought you'd want to go up again. You said you wanted to learn to fly, and I said I'd teach you. If you want an apology, all you have to do is give me a reasonable explanation."

"I've spent enough time explaining myself to you. More than you deserve. Questions, always questions. Never *trust.*" Her eyes smoldered with blue fire. "I want you to leave my room. I want you to leave me alone for the rest of the time I have in my father's house."

"You had me going." His fingers tightened on her arms, and she caught her breath at the pressure. "I bought it all. The big, innocent eyes, the virginal frailty, the pictures you painted of a woman looking for her father's affection and nothing else. *Trust?*" he flung back at her. "You'd taken me to the point where I trusted you more than myself. You knew I wanted you, and you worked on me. All those trembles and melting bones and artless looks. You played it perfectly, right down to the blushes." He pulled her against him, nearly lifting her off her feet.

"Dillon, you're hurting me." She faltered.

"I wanted you," he went on, as if she had not spoken. "Last night I was aching for you, but I treated you with a restraint and respect I've never shown another woman. You slip on that innocent aura that drives a man crazy. You shouldn't have used it on me, Duchess."

Terror shivered along her skin. Her breath was rapid and aching in her lungs.

"Game's over. I'm going to collect." He silenced her protest with a hard, punishing kiss. Though she struggled against his imprisoning arms, she made no more ripple than a leaf battling a whirlpool. The room tilted, and she was crushed beneath him on the mattress. She fought against the intimacy as his mouth and hands bruised her. He was claiming her in fury, disposing of the barrier of her robe and possessing her flesh with angry demand.

Slowly, his movements altered in texture. Punishment became seduction as his hands began to caress rather than bruise. His mouth left hers to trail down her throat. With a sob ending on a moan, Laine surrendered. Her body became pliant under his, her will snapping with the weight of sensations never tasted. Tears gathered, but she made no more effort to halt them than she did the man who urged them from her soul.

All movement stopped abruptly, and Dillon lay still. The room was thrown into a tortured silence, broken only by the sound of quick breathing. Lifting his head, Dillon studied the journey of a tear down Laine's cheek. He swore with sudden eloquence, then rose. He tugged a hand through his hair as he turned this back on her.

"This is the first time I've been driven to nearly forcing myself on a woman." His voice was low and harsh as he swung around and stared at her. Laine lay still, emotionally drained. She made no effort to cover herself, but merely stared up at him with the eyes of a wounded child. "I can't deal with what you do to me, Laine."

Turning on his heel, he strode from the room. Laine thought the slamming of her door the loneliest sound she had ever heard.

Chapter Twelve

It was raining on the new spring grass. From her dormitory window Laine watched the green brighten with its morning bath. Outside her door, she heard girls trooping down the hall toward breakfast, but she did not smile at their gay chattering in French and English. She found smiles still difficult.

It had not yet been two weeks since Miri had met Laine's packed cases with a frown and drawn brows. She had met Laine's sketchy explanations with crossed arms and further questions. Laine had remained firm, refusing to postpone her departure or to give specific answers. The note she had left for her father had contained no more details, only an apology for her abrupt leave-taking and a promise to write once she had settled back in France. As of yet, Laine had not found the courage to put pen to paper.

Memories of her last moments with Dillon continued to haunt her. She could still smell the perfume of island blossoms, still feel the warm, moist air rise from the sea to move over her skin. Watching the moon wane, she could remember its lush fullness over the heads of palms. She had hoped her memories would fade with time. She reminded herself that Kauai and its promises were behind her.

It's better this way, she told herself, picking up her brush and preparing herself for the day's work. *Better for everyone*. Her father was settled in his life and would be content to exchange occasional letters. One day, perhaps, he would visit her. Laine knew she could never go back. She, too, had her own life, a job, the comfort of familiar surroundings. Here, she knew what was expected of her. Her existence would be tranquil and unmarred by storms of emotions. She closed her eyes on Dillon's image.

It's too soon, she told herself. Too soon to test her ability to think of him without pain. Later, when the memory had dulled, she would open the door. When she allowed herself to think of him again, it would be to remember the beauty.

It was easier to forget if she followed a routine. Laine scheduled each day to allow for a minimum of idle time. Classes claimed her mornings and early afternoons, and she spent the remainder of her days with chores designed to keep her mind and hands busy.

Throughout the day, the rain continued. With a musical plop, the inevitable leak dripped into the basin on Laine's classroom floor. The school building was old and rambling. Repairs were always either just completed, slated to be done or in vague consideration for the future. The windows were shut against the damp, but the gloom crept into the room. The students were languid and inattentive. Her final class of the day was made up of English girls just entering adolescence. They were thoroughly bored by their hour lesson on French grammar. As it was Saturday, there was only a half day of classes, but the hours dragged. Hugging her navy blazer closer, Laine reflected that the afternoon would be better employed with a good book and a cheerful fire than by conjugating verbs in a rain-dreary classroom.

"Eloise," Laine said, recalling her duty. "One must postpone naps until after class."

The girl's eyes blinked open. She gave a groggy, self-conscious smile as her classmates giggled. "Yes, Mademoiselle Simmons."

Laine bit back a sigh. "You will have your freedom in ten minutes," she reminded them as she perched on the edge of her desk. "If you have forgotten, it is Saturday. Sunday follows."

This information brought murmurs of approval and a few straightened shoulders. Seeing she had at least momentarily captured their attention, Laine went on. "*Maintenant*, the verb *chanter*. To sing. *Attendez, ensuite répétez. Je chante, tu chantes, il chante, nous chantons, vous* . . ." Her voice faded as she saw the man leaning against the open door in the rear of the classroom.

"*Vous chantez.*"

Laine forced her attention back to young Eloise. "*Oui, vous chantez, et ils chantent. Répétez.*"

Obediently, the music of high girlish voices repeated the lesson. Laine retreated behind her desk while Dillon stood calmly and watched. As the voices faded into silence, Laine wracked her brain for the assignment she had planned.

"*Bien.* You will write, for Monday, sentences using this verb in all its forms. Eloise, we will not consider '*Il chante*' an imaginative sentence."

"Yes, Mademoiselle Simmons."

The bell rang signaling the end of class.

"You will not run," she called over the furious clatter of shuffling desks and scurrying feet. Gripping her hands in her lap, Laine prepared herself for the encounter.

She watched the girls giggle and whisper as they passed by Dillon, and saw, as her heart spun circles, his familiar, easy grin. Crossing the room with his long stride, he stood before her.

"Hello, Dillon." She spoke quickly to cover her confusion. "You seem to have quite an effect on my students."

He studied her in silence as she fought to keep her smile in place. The flood of emotion threatened to drown her.

"You haven't changed," he said at length. "I don't know why I was afraid you would." Reaching in his pocket, he pulled out the locket and placed it on her desk. Unable to speak, Laine stared at it. As her eyes filled, her hand closed convulsively over the gold heart. "Not a very eloquent apology, but I haven't had a lot of practice. For pity's sake, Laine." His tone shifted into anger so quickly, she lifted her head in shock. "If you needed money, why didn't you tell me?"

"And confirm your opinion of my character?" she retorted.

Turning away, Dillon moved to a window and looked into the insistent mist of rain. "I had that one coming," he murmured, then rested his hands on the sill and lapsed into silence.

She was moved by the flicker of pain that had crossed his face. "There's no purpose in recriminations now, Dillon. It's best to leave all that in the past." Rising, she kept the desk between them. "I'm very grateful to you for taking the time and the trouble to return my locket. It's more important to me than I can tell you. I don't know when I'll be able to pay you. I . . ."

Dillon whirled, and Laine stepped away from the fury on his face. She watched him struggle for control. "No, don't say anything, just give me a minute." His hands retreated to his pockets. For several long moments, he paced the room. Gradually, his movements grew calmer. "The roof leaks," he said idly.

"Only when it rains."

He gave a short laugh and turned back to her. "Maybe it doesn't mean much, but I'm sorry. No." He shook his head to ward her off as she began to answer. "Don't be so blasted generous. It'll only make me more guilty." He started to light a cigarette, remembered where he was and let out a long breath. "After my exhibition of stupidity, I went up for a while. I find that I think more clearly a few thousand feet off the ground. You might find this hard to believe, and I suppose it's even more ridiculous to expect you to forgive me, but I did manage to get a grip on reality. I didn't even believe the things I was saying to you when I was saying them." He rubbed his hands over his face, and Laine noticed for the first time that he looked tired and drawn. "I only know that I went a little crazy from the first minute I saw you.

"I went back to the house with the intention of offering a series of inadequate apologies. I tried to rationalize that all the accusations I tossed at you about Cap were made for his sake." He shook his head, and a faint smile touched his mouth. "It didn't help."

"Dillon . . ."

"Laine, don't interrupt. I haven't the patience as it is." He paced again, and she stood silent. "I'm not very good at this, so just don't say anything until I'm finished." Restless, he continued to roam around the room as he spoke. "When I got back, Miri was waiting for me. I couldn't get anything out of her at first but a detailed lecture on my character. Finally, she told me you'd gone. I didn't take that news very well, but it's no use going into that now. After a lot of glaring and ancient curses, she told me about the locket. I had to swear a blood oath not to tell Cap. It seems you had her word on that. I've been in France for ten days trying to find you." Turning back, he gestured in frustration. "Ten days," he repeated as if it were a lifetime. "It wasn't until this morning that I traced the maid who worked for your mother. She was very expansive once I settled her into broken English. I got an earful about debts and auctions and the little mademoiselle who stayed in school over Christmas vacations while Madame went to San Moritz. She gave me the name of your school." Dillon paused. For a moment there was only the sound of water dripping from the ceiling into the basin. "There's nothing you can say to me that I haven't already said to myself, in more graphic terms. But I figured you should have the chance."

Seeing he was finished, Laine drew a deep breath and prepared to speak. "Dillon, I've thought carefully on how my position would have looked to you. You knew only one side, and your heart was with my father. I find it difficult, when I'm calm, to resent that loyalty or your protection of his welfare. As for what happened on the last morning—" Laine swallowed, striving to keep her voice composed. "I think it was as difficult for you as it was for me, perhaps more difficult."

"You'd make it a whole lot easier on my conscience if you'd yell or toss a few things at me."

"I'm sorry." She managed a smile and lifted her shoulders with the apology. "I'd have to be very angry to do that, especially here. The nuns frown on displays of temper."

"Cap wants you to come home."

Laine's smile faded at his quiet words. He watched her eyes go bleak before she shook her head and moved to the window. "This is my home."

"Your home's on Kauai. Cap wants you back. Is it fair for him to lose you twice?"

"Is it fair to ask me to turn my back on my own life and return?" she countered, trying to block out the pain his words were causing. "Don't talk to me about fair, Dillon."

"Look, be as bitter as you want about me. I

deserve it. Cap doesn't. How do you think he feels knowing what your childhood was like?"

"You told him?" She whirled around, and for the first time since he had come into the room, Dillon saw her mask of control slip. "You had no right . . ."

"I had every right," he interrupted. "Just as Cap had every right to know. Laine, listen to me." She had started to turn away, but his words and quiet tone halted her. "He loves you. He never stopped, not all those years. I guess that's why I reacted to you the way I did." With an impatient sound, he ran his hands through his hair again. "For fifteen years loving you hurt him."

"Don't you think I know that?" she tossed back. "Why must he be hurt more?"

"Laine, the few days you were with him gave him back his daughter. He didn't ask why you never answered his letters, he never accused you of any of the things I did." He shut his eyes briefly, and again she noticed fatigue. "He loved you without needing explanations or apologies. It would have been wrong to prolong the lies. When he found you'd left, he wanted to come to France himself to bring you back. I asked him to let me come alone because I knew it was my fault that you left."

"There's no blame, Dillon." With a sigh, Laine slipped the locket into her blazer pocket. "Perhaps you were right to tell Cap. Perhaps it's cleaner. I'll write him myself tonight; it was wrong of me to leave without seeing him. Knowing that he is really my father again is the greatest gift I've ever had. I don't want either one of you to think that my living in France means I hold any resentment. I very much hope that Cap visits me soon. Perhaps you'd carry a note back for me."

Dillon's eyes darkened. His voice was tight with anger when he spoke. "He isn't going to like knowing you're buried in this school."

Laine turned away from him and faced the window.

"I'm not buried, Dillon. The school is my home and my job."

"And your escape?" he demanded impatiently, then swore as he saw her stiffen. He began to pace again. "I'm sorry, that was a cheap shot."

"No more apologies, Dillon. I don't believe the floors can stand the wear."

He stopped his pacing and studied her. Her back was still to him, but he could just see the line of her chin against the pale cap of curls. In the trim navy blazer and white pleated skirt, she looked more student than teacher. He began to speak in a lighter tone. "Listen, Duchess, I'm going to stay around for a couple of days, play tourist. How about showing me around? I could use someone who speaks the language."

Laine shut her eyes, thinking of what a few days in his company would mean. There was no point in prolonging the pain. "I'm sorry,

Dillon, I'd love to take you around, but I haven't the time at the moment. My work here has backed up since I took the time off to visit Kauai."

"You're going to make this difficult, aren't you?"

"I'm not trying to do that, Dillon." Laine turned with an apologetic smile. "Another time, perhaps."

"I haven't got another time. I'm trying my best to do this right, but I'm not sure of my moves. I've never dealt with a woman like you before. All the rules are different." She saw, with curiosity, that his usual confidence had vanished. He took a step toward her, stopped, then walked to the blackboard. For some moments, he studied the conjugation of several French verbs. "Have dinner with me tonight."

"No, Dillon, I . . ." He whirled around so swiftly, Laine swallowed the rest of her words.

"If you won't even have dinner with me, how the devil am I supposed to talk you into coming home so I can struggle through this courting routine? Any fool could see I'm no good at this sort of thing. I've already made a mess of it. I don't know how much longer I can stand here and be reasonably coherent. I love you, Laine, and it's driving me crazy. Come back to Kauai so we can be married."

Stunned into speechlessness, Laine stared at him. "Dillon," she began, "did you say you love me?"

"Yes, I said I love you. Do you want to hear it again?" His hands descended to her shoulders, his lips to her hair. "I love you so much I'm barely able to do simple things like eat and sleep for thinking of you. I keep remembering how you looked with a shell held to your ear. You stood there with the water running from your hair, and your eyes the color of the sky and the sea, and I fell completely in love with you. I tried not to believe it, but I lost ground every time you got near me. When you left, it was like losing part of myself. I'm not complete anymore without you."

"Dillon." His name was only a whisper.

"I swore I wasn't going to put any pressure on you." She felt his brow lower to the crown of her head. "I wasn't going to say all these things to you at once like this. I'll give you whatever you need, the flowers, the candlelight. You'd be surprised how conventional I can be when it's necessary. Just come back with me, Laine. I'll give you some time before I start pressuring you to marry me."

"No." She shook her head, then took a deep breath. "I won't come back with you unless you marry me first."

"Listen." Dillon tightened his grip, then with a groan of pleasure lowered his mouth to hers. "You drive a hard bargain," he murmured as he tasted her lips. As if starved for the flavor, he lingered over the kiss.

"I'm not going to give you the opportunity to change your mind." Lifting her arms, Laine circled his neck, then laid her cheek against his. "You can give me the flowers and candlelight after we're married."

"Duchess, you've got a deal. I'll have you married to me before you realize what you're getting into. Some people might tell you I have a few faults—such as, I occasionally lose my temper—"

"Really? Laine lifted an incredulous face. "I've never known anyone more mild and even tempered. However"—she trailed her finger down his throat and toyed with the top button of his shirt—"I suppose I should confess that I am by nature very jealous. It's just something I can't control. And if I ever see another woman dance the hula especially for you, I shall probably throw her off the nearest cliff!"

"Would you?" Dillon gave a self-satisfied masculine grin as he framed her face in his hands. "Then I think Miri should start teaching you as soon as we get back. I warn you, I plan to sit in on every lesson."

"I'm sure I'll be a quick learner." Rising to her toes, Laine pulled him closer. "But right now there are other things I would rather learn. Kiss me again, Dillon!"

Silhouette Romance

READERS' COMMENTS ON SILHOUETTE ROMANCES:

"I would like to congratulate you on the most wonderful books I've had the pleasure of reading. They are a tremendous joy to those of us who have yet to meet the man of our dreams. From reading your books I quite truly believe that he will someday appear before me like a prince!"

—L.L.*, Hollandale, MS

"Your books are great, wholesome fiction, always with an upbeat, happy ending. Thank you."

—M.D., Massena, NY

"My boyfriend always teases me about Silhouette Books. He asks me, how's my love life and naturally I say terrific, but I tell him that there is always room for a little more romance from Silhouette."

—F.N., Ontario, Canada

"I would like to sincerely express my gratitude to you and your staff for bringing the pleasure of your publications to my attention. Your books are well written, mature and very contemporary."

—D.D., Staten Island, NY

*names available on request